17 $\frac{00}{}$

YADULT PZ 7 .W78436 HAR 1999
Wittlinger, Ellen.
Hard love

NORTHAMPTON COMMUNITY COLLEGE
LIBRARY
Bethlehem PA 18020

Hard Love

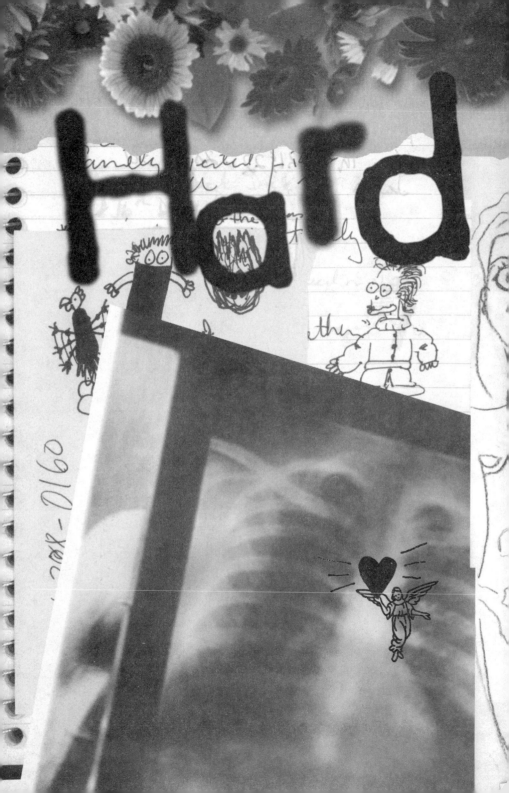

LOVE

ellen wittlinger

NORTHAMPTON
LIBRARY
Bethlehem, PA 18020
COMMUNITY COLLEGE

Simon & Schuster

SIMON & SCHUSTER BOOKS FOR YOUNG READERS

 An imprint of Simon & Schuster Children's Publishing Division
1230 Avenue of the Americas, New York, New York 10020

Text copyright © 1999 by Ellen Wittlinger
All rights reserved including the right of reproduction in whole or in part in any form.
SIMON & SCHUSTER BOOKS FOR YOUNG READERS is a trademark of Simon & Schuster.
Lyrics on page 110 are from "Names & Dates & Times" by Ani DiFranco.
© 1993 Righteous Babe Records—BMI. All rights reserved. Used by permission.
Lyrics on pages 212-213 are from "Hard Love" by Bob Franke.
© 1982 Telephone Pole Music Co. Used by permission.
Book design by Heather Wood / The text for this book is set in Legacy Sans Medium.
Printed and bound in the United States of America.
10   9   8   7   6   5   4

Library of Congress Cataloging-in-Publication Data
Wittlinger, Ellen.
Hard love / Ellen Wittlinger. — 1st ed.
p.   cm.
Summary: After starting to publish a zine in which he writes his secret feelings about
his lonely life and his parents' divorce, sixteen-year-old John meets an unusual girl
and begins to develop a healthier personality.   ISBN 0-689-82134-4
[1. Authorship—Fiction. 2. Underground press publications—Fiction. 3. Divorce—Fiction.
4. Identity—Fiction.] I. Title.
PZ7.W78436Har 1999   [Fic]—dc21   98-6668   CIP   AC

For Kate and Morgan

And for everyone
whose first love
was a hard love.

With many thanks to the zine writers
who gave me advice and a glimpse into their world:

Colette Ryder-Hall (Looks Yellow, Tastes Red)
W. Lugh Van Droog (Lugh Spoke)
Amanda Hughes (Paranoy)
Ariel Bordeaux (Deep Girl)
Neil Simon (Gobstopper and automaton)
Ellen Myre (Noisemaker)
Ski-Mask (Riverside Art Scene)

Thanks also to my editor, David Gale, and to my agent, Ginger Knowlton.

And special thanks to Ani DiFranco and Bob Franke
for their generosity in the use of their lyrics.

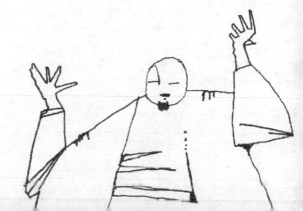

Hard Love

Chapter One

I am immune to emotion. I have been ever since I can remember. Which is helpful when people appeal to my sympathy. I don't seem to have any.

"Come on, John. It's not going to kill you to go to the auditions with me," Brian begged. "I hate doing stuff alone." He walked backward to the door of Darlington High's Little Theater, beckoning to me as though I were his golden retriever.

"Look," I told him, "I can't sing, I can't act, and I don't like musicals anyway. Especially this one. It's sappy." I didn't bother to remind him that I don't really go to this school. People think I do, but it's only my physical body, not *me*. Brian can't seem to understand that.

"You think *The Sound of Music* is sappy? It's about the rise of the Third Reich! It's about standing up for your beliefs..."

"It's about the hills are alive and singing nuns." As if Brian knows squat about standing up for your beliefs anyway. Brian's most strongly held belief is that having a girlfriend will make him a viable human being, but let a girl say hi to him in the hallway and his knees buckle.

"How come you're suddenly so interested in drama?" I asked him, though I didn't really care. "You never tried out for a play before."

Brian's acne turned wine red, which was his charming way of blushing. He glanced quickly up and down the corridor. "*She's* trying out. She always gets a big part in the musicals, and everybody says she'll get the lead this time."

Jesus. "Who?" I asked, just to annoy him.

Brian rolled his eyes and leaned in close. "*Violet Neville*," he whispered. He was so damn close to me he breathed her nauseatingly sweet name right into my mouth.

"How old are you?" I asked, backing away.

"Whataya mean?"

"I mean you've been dreaming about that useless girl since the sixth grade. Six years, Brian. Get a life! You've never even spoken to her!"

"I have too!"

"You have not. You think just because you get some minuscule part in this play she's suddenly going to notice you? You think Fräulein Maria is going to fall in love with Nazi Soldier Number Six?"

Brian looked squashed, which, I have to admit, was the look I was after. I'm really a pretty crappy friend. "I didn't say that. At least I'll get to be around her. They rehearse after school every day for the next two months."

The thing is, it makes me feel sick when Brian acts like this. Hangdog—that's the word for it, and accurate, too. Like one of those skinny mutts that can't even hold up its tail, the kind that follows you around on the street whining and panting, and you can't imagine what combination of canine breeds could be behind such a pathetic specimen.

I just had to bail. "Look, I gotta go. I've got something to do this afternoon."

"Right," Brian said sarcastically. "*Your* life's so full. You don't even have a *dream* girl."

I had to laugh, which probably wasn't the response Brian was expecting. But I don't mind him zinging me back. It's the only reason we're friends at all. We recognized each other the first day we met—two hollow souls trying to pass for normal. Together we still add up to zero, but at least our hopelessness has a twin. It works well enough. I don't mind hanging around with a kindly fool, and Brian doesn't mind hanging around with a witty misanthrope. And it appears to the world as if we each have at least *one* friend.

Of course, I hadn't bothered to tell Brian that lately my life didn't seem quite so yawningly empty as before. He wouldn't understanding that reading things somebody wrote in a magazine could change you.

"Call me later, if you want to," I said. It was the least I could do. "Let me know how it goes."

"Screw you," Brian said, and turned to go into the theater, his head drooping onto his chest, tail between his legs. At least he was still swearing at me. That was a good sign.

Interview with the Stepfather

BOY: So, you'd like to interview for the job of stepfather?

STEP: Well, I will if I have to. I sure would like to marry your mother.

BOY: And I'd sure like to know your qualifications for the job, if I may.

STEP: I didn't think I needed any qualifications. I mean, the real job is being a husband to your mother, isn't it? This stepfather thing just happens. I didn't think I'd have to do anything.

BOY: You don't *have* to, however, doing nothing would make you indistinguishable from my real father. Surely you don't want that to happen.

STEP: Oh, certainly not. I'm glad you told me. Well, if he doesn't do anything, I guess that means I'll have to do a lot. What kinds of things should I do, though? Take you to baseball games? Toss the old football around the yard? You like to go fishing?

BOY: God, no. How about if you help me pull a few tricks on Mom? Maybe we could put some plastic cockroaches in her bed, or fill her shampoo bottle with maple syrup, or donate all her shoes to the Salvation Army? I think it would help us bond.

STEP: What! I would never do that to your mother! What's the matter with you, Boy?

BOY: I guess I just need a firm but loving hand.

STEP: You do, young fella, and I'll be there to give it to you.

BOY: I'm sure you will. I'm sure you gave it to your own son, didn't you?

STEP: My son? Well, I don't see the boy too often. Lives in another state, you know.

BOY: State of confusion?

STEP: Huh?

BOY: Let's continue with the interview: Are you aware that when my beloved mother snores it measures six point two on the Richter scale? And did you know that when the cat bit her, she bit him back?

STEP: Stop it, Boy. You're lying. You don't deserve to have such a wonderful mother, if you don't mind my saying so.

BOY: Don't mind in the least. I'd even agree with you. She, however, does deserve me. After all, that wonderful mother raised me, didn't she? Molded me into the great guy I am today. What you see before you is the result of her hard work.

STEP: You know what I think? I think you must be just like your dad. It's not your mother's fault you're so rotten—it's that lousy father of yours.

BOY: Sir, I think you hit the nail on the head. I'm a reproduction of the old bore: selfish and full of shit. The prize for your insightfulness is the hand of my mother. Long may it wave.

STEP: Get lost, kid. We don't need your kind 'round here.

BOY: My feelings exactly.

I don't know what it means really—it's not how I'd ever talk to Mom's dishwater-drab boyfriend Al—but I like the way it sounds. It's true, even though it never happened. That's what I love about writing. Once you get the words down on paper, in print, they start to make sense. It's like you don't know what you think until it dribbles from your brain down your arm and into your hand and out through your fingers and shows up on the computer screen, and you read it and realize: That's really true; I believe that.

Typed up *Interview* filled three pages of my zine, which brought the total number of pages to twelve. Not as long as some of the zines I'd seen, but long enough for a first issue. Especially since I still had to get it copied and stapled by tomorrow night before Dad came to pick me up for the weekend.

I'm not much of an artist, so the cover looks a little cheap. Just the title, *Bananafish*, in fancy letters that took me hours to draw, and a photocopy of an old picture of me when I was three years old, sitting behind a birthday cake screaming my head off. The picture would be grainy when I copied it again, but that was okay. Zines were supposed to look like that, homemade and weird.

I thumbed through my copy of *Escape Velocity* one more time to see if there was anything I'd forgotten. This was the most incredible zine of all the ones I picked up the past few months at Tower Records. Although the cover was fancier than mine with the kind of clip art and newspaper headlines and crazy drawings that you usually see in zines, inside was mostly writing, wild, funny writing about all kinds of stuff.

The author, somebody named Marisol, has this electric brain that leaps from one subject to another, each one stranger than the last. She claims to be seventeen, but she sounds much too cool to still be in high school.

She wrote about walking in the cemetery and imagining old dead families still arguing, lying underground and berating each other over whose fault it was that Junior never made a go of the business, or why Eleanor, though a beauty, had been unlucky in love. She gave a list of Shakespearean insults and begged her readers to call each other "hasty-witted pontificating footlickers," so as to put some "grit and romance" back into the English language.

There was an article called "Why My Mother Still Has a Dorothy Hamill Haircut," which actually had me laughing out loud, which goes against my basic instincts. The gist of this one was that her mother wants to remind people that Dorothy Hamill (some Olympic ice-skater from the seventies) should still be their role model. "Mom is on a mission to convince girlkind that big thighs don't count against you as long as you smile shyly up at folks through a swingy wave of clean hair. She would tell you (if she were here) that a good blunt cut draws the eye away from a low center of gravity." It goes on like that for pages.

Then there was a page titled "Why My Father Still Watches Lawrence Welk Reruns on Cable." That was at the top of the page, then halfway down, in the middle of all this white space, it says, "Sometimes the truth is unknowable."

My favorite piece didn't even have a title. It was on the first page and it just started right out:

My name is Marisol, which means "bitter sun." But I am not bitter because that would be a waste of my time, and wasting time is one of the only sins worth worrying about. Marisol, so I'm told, is a very popular name in Puerto Rico, where I have never been. My birth parents were Puerto Rican, and because my adoptive mother, the white Yankee social worker, is particularly sensitive to these kinds of issues, she named me according to my heritage. My adoptive father was born in Cuba, but came to the U.S. when he was twelve. No one is more American than my Cuban college professor daddy. Adopting me was small potatoes after adopting a new country, a new language, new loyalties, new life. And so I became Marisol Guzman, Puerto Rican Cuban Yankee Cambridge, Massachusetts, rich spoiled lesbian private-school gifted-and-talented writer virgin looking for love.

God! When you read something like that you can't help but believe it. I mean, it's not just some smartass trying to impress you with some baloney. I really have to admire the way Marisol just lays her life out for people to see, like she loves the weird way she is, and if you had any sense, you would too. Every time I read that over, I feel like I'm looking down through layer after layer of her, until I'm looking more deeply inside this person I don't even know than I've ever looked inside myself. I want to write like that too. Maybe I even want to *be* like that. And I sure as hell want to meet her.

The only thing I still needed to do was put my name on the cover and I'd be finished with my zine. But who was I? Marisol might not be her real name. Maybe she just liked that stuff about the "bitter sun." Like I said, you can be "true" without always telling the truth. People use made-up names for their zines all the time, names like Ratty and Tanker and Whizzer. No way was I going to put "by John F. Galardi Jr." John Galardi sounded like some dull stiff, some nerd extraordinaire who couldn't get out of his own way. And that Jr. thing I never used. What's that about, anyway? It's like telling your kid, "You're just a smaller version of me, Son. You're not really *worth* a name of your own."

So, I was thinking I might use "Giovanni." Why not? One name, foreign, unusual, memorable, but still, almost my real name—if only I'd been born in Italy instead of Darlington, Mass. I inked it in carefully at the bottom of the cover, all the letters slanted backward like these cool dudes walking.

"Mom, I need the car for a little while, okay?" God, she

was sitting in the dark again. I thought that was over with now that she had Al to replace Dad. She'd spent the better part of five years, evenings anyway, sitting on that scratchy old couch in the dark. "Resting" is what she called it, but it seemed to me more like burying herself alive. But then, this past winter the lights went on again, which had been a relief mostly, except that now there was usually this bald guy sitting on the couch next to her, pretty damn close too, grinning like a skinhead Mr. Rogers.

"It's awfully late to go out, Johnny," she said. She'd say it was awfully late to go out if it was noon.

"It's only eight thirty. I have to get something copied for school tomorrow. Where's Al?"

"He's not coming over tonight. I'm...thinking about things."

"You didn't...? He's not...?" God, if that creep dumped her...

"No. It's not that." She reached out and switched on a lamp, which made us both blink. "The thing is, Al asked me to marry him." A twitchy smile kept coming and going while she talked.

"Oh." No surprise—I figured it was coming. And what the hell were you supposed to say when your mother made an announcement like that? "I knew he would. I mean, he seems like the type who'd want to get married. He was married before."

She kept on twitching. "Yup, we're both used goods."

"Oh, Mom." I started booting the wall with my sneaker. Damn! I hated it when she said stuff like that, feel-

ing so sorry for herself. People got divorced all the time. Practically everybody I knew had divorced parents. Lots of them anyway. It was a fact of life. Why couldn't she get used to it? I had.

"I don't know what to do," she said. "He's been wonderful to me. I thought my life was over, but Al brought me back."

More yuck. I also couldn't stand it when she got confidential with me; I really didn't want to know more than I had to about her relationship with old Al. "Well, I guess you'd better marry the guy then," I said.

She laughed. "Easy for you to say. Ever heard the saying, 'Once burned, twice shy'?"

"No." How much of this conversation should I have to endure just to drive the car half a mile?

She picked a piece of hard candy from the dish on the coffee table and twisted the cellophane tighter around the sour ball. "If I marry him, I'm leaving myself wide open again. What's to stop him from doing the same thing your father did?"

I banged the manila envelope against my leg. "Mom, the store's gonna close. Could we discuss this another time?"

She stared at me, but I had the feeling she was seeing somebody else, maybe somebody standing right behind me. It creeped me out a little bit. "We used to be close when you were younger. Before things got bad with your father. Do you remember?"

"Mom," I whined. I wished I could disappear when she got onto these topics.

"Now you can't give me five minutes of your precious time. Whom am I supposed to talk to about this? My fifth grade class?"

"What do you want me to say? I hardly know the guy. How can I tell you what to do?"

"Al's tried to get to know you."

"Look, I don't have time to get to know people, okay? Al's already got a son and I've already got a father. Why complicate things?"

She sighed and looked unhappy, which was nothing new. But, of course, I'm immune to it. "Keys are in my coat pocket in the hall. Drive carefully. The life you save may be mine."

Thou scurvy tickle-brained hell-hated lunatic.

Thou lascivious weather-bitten flap-ear'd
strumpet.

Thou churlish fen-sucked maggot pie.

Thou dizzy-eyed hedge-born canker-blossom.

Thou puppy-headed beslubbering flax-wench.

Thou peevish ill-nurtured milksop.

That last one fit me pretty well. *Peevish ill-nurtured milk-sop.* Marisol had made up a list of insults using Shakespearean language for which I could imagine numerous possible uses. It made the insults even better that the insul-

tees wouldn't have a clue what you were saying. You could mix and match to suit the situation. I could think of several beslubbering fen-sucked canker-blossoms I now had the vocabulary to slander.

The more I read her stuff, the more I couldn't wait to meet Marisol. And I would too, as long as she was telling the truth on the inside cover of *Escape Velocity* #1. "If you like this zine and would like to have issue #2, send one dollar and two stamps to the address below, or stop by Tower Records on Newbury Street after Saturday, March 2. Free copies in the entryway." The address was a post office box in Cambridge, but the other information surely meant that she would be bringing the zine to Tower Records sometime Saturday when I would be there waiting.

I flipped to the back page of *Escape Velocity* and read again, for probably the twentieth time, the definition of the zine's title. "Escape velocity: the speed at which a body must travel to escape the gravitational pull of another body." I loved thinking about it—that moment when you got free, when you were going so fast you left them all behind. And I kept picturing this girl, Marisol, large and muscular probably, outrunning a tornado or something, jumping off a garage roof and actually flying.

"Your copies are ready, kid." The woman leaned across the counter to look at me sitting on the floor. "Fifty. Fresh and warm."

I stood up as she rang the numbers into the machine.

"You a writer?" she asked me. "You write this stuff?"

"Yeah."

"Who'd you write it for? Your girlfriend?"

Who would ask a total stranger a nosy question like that? People were always saying stuff that made you wonder if they'd ever had a successful conversation in their lives.

"No," I said. "I don't have a girlfriend. I wrote it for anybody who wants to read it. I wrote it for myself."

She shook her head, but smiled. "Kids," she said, as though she had a special insight into the species; then, as I tucked the pages under my arm to leave, she kept the nightly news coming. "Good luck, Giovanni," she said. "You're a good kid." Now, where the hell does she get off saying something like that?

Chapter Two

It was eleven already. I'd been standing in the entryway since the minute the store opened at ten o'clock, and I was beginning to feel pretty conspicuous. One of the clerks behind the counter kept giving me suspicious looks. I considered sitting down and reading one of the other zines stacked around me so I looked like I was doing something useful, but what if I got absorbed in an article and Marisol came in, dropped off the new *Escape Velocity*s and took off before I realized it?

My stack of *Bananafish* copies looked pretty low-budget compared to some of the stuff piled on the floor. Still, a couple of kids had come by and picked one up along with a few other zines. I didn't say anything. For instance, I didn't say, "I wrote that one," like some egotistical dork who thinks he's a celebrity because he stapled some pages together. My address was inside; they could write me a note and tell me if they liked it. Or if they hated it—that could happen, too.

I looked out the window trying to guess which people might be coming into the store, which girl might be Marisol. But as people kept zooming past I got a headache, a twin to the one I had the night before at dinner. Of course, that was nothing new; I always got a headache on Friday nights, but it usually lifted as soon as my father dropped me off at his condo in Back Bay and left. Good old Dad always manages to have pressing commitments on weekend nights: charity benefits, literary events, parties given by important people he can't afford to miss. Every week. What a joke.

Probably at least half the time he's just on a regular old date (if that's even what you call it when people are that old), but he probably thinks a date isn't a good enough excuse for running out on his only kid. It's true the guy almost never misses a Friday night dinner—that's his penance, to spend an hour a week face to face with me. But once the torture of eating pizza together is over, we're both free to spend the rest of the weekend as we please. Sometimes I barely glimpse him again until we get into the Saab Sunday afternoon for the drive back to Darlington.

Of course, I never tell my mom this; she assumes we spend the whole weekend together. She'd be bullshit if she knew. It's easy to lie because she never questions me about Dad. It suits my purposes that they know nothing about each other anymore; it gives me some privacy.

I guess Mom doesn't really want to know how chummy we two guys are. Once in a while she gets a little curious, but all I have to do is make up a simple story about a movie

or a basketball game and she's satisfied. One time, when I was younger, I told her an elaborate lie for no particular reason, just to see if I could get away with it, I guess, about a party Dad had taken me to and how I'd met all these dancers from the Boston Ballet and some actors from the American Repertory Theater. I even mentioned a few famous painters whose names I remembered from books that had been lying around on Dad's coffee table for two or three years, books published by his company. Mom got that familiar twitch in her face when I mentioned the names, and her eyes got wet too, maybe because those were the kinds of people she used to meet when she and Dad went out together, or maybe just because now she knew for certain her son was a heartless liar. I'm not sure. But after that I made my lies smaller and less interesting.

I certainly never mention to her how often Dad has girlfriends over to spend the night. I try not to know too much about that myself. I mean, Dad has outfitted this room for me with a TV, a VCR, a CD player, a computer, and a refrigerator, obviously hoping I'll never have a reason to leave it. Unfortunately, I still have to go to the bathroom now and then, but I always check the whereabouts of all other guests before making a late night dash.

Up until a few months ago Brian sometimes came into Boston with me for the weekend. It was easier to have somebody else there when I was younger, when I still felt anger balled up in the back of my throat every time Dad asked me a question. Brian would chatter away about dumb stuff, like why his mother bought kosher hot dogs even though they weren't Jewish, and Dad and I would just sit there bored silly, but at least we didn't have to speak to each other. But lately we've gotten more comfortable with our own meaningless conversations, or, more often, silence.

Besides, this year Brian has become a maniac about girls, and it really gets on my nerves. Brian thinks the female population of Boston is much cooler than the girls in Darlington (with the exception of the extraordinary Violet Neville, of course). He can go on about it for hours. We'll be walking down Newbury Street, which is always full of girls—everything from hippie students to model wannabes—and Brian will be practically panting.

"Do you think that girl's pretty? Do you like nose rings? Don't you think she looks like that girl on *Party of Five*? Do you think Michelle Pfeiffer is more beautiful than Claudia Schiffer? If you could go out with any model, which one would you pick? Don't you think red hair makes a girl look hot?"

I can't stand it anymore, the constant talk about girls and sex. I just don't feel like thinking about that stuff. Maybe it's weird, but I'm not interested in it. I mean, it worries me a little sometimes, because I guess guys my age are supposed to be like Brian, lusting after pouty lips and big boobs. But to me, the mystery of female body parts is one I'd just as soon not solve. Not that I'm interested in boys either—I'm just not interested in the whole idea of locked lips or proclamations of love. I can't imagine being in love with somebody, letting her touch me and tell me things I wouldn't know whether to believe.

I'm starting to think I'll probably never have a girl-friend, which would be okay too. On those few occasions when a girl has actually flirted with me, tipped her head sideways and laughed at some stupid remark, all it did was make me angry. It seemed like she was playing a game with idiotic rules. First you laugh, then you tell a pretty lie, then you stick your tongue in each other's mouths, then you say something really mean and hurtful to each other, then you go off to find somebody else who wants to play the game. This is an activity for intelligent people? I think not.

It's kind of unfair, but I think I probably *could* have a girlfriend (if I wanted one) more easily than Brian. Not only does the guy turn into a stuttering sweatbox around females, but he also carries about 120 pounds on six feet of bones. He's got this incredibly curly brown hair that sticks way out so that altogether he looks like a little kid's draw-ing of a tree. Whereas I actually look fairly normal: average height and weight, a pretty low zit count, and straight black hair just long enough to appear slightly unkempt (the I-don't-give-a-damn look). Freshman year a girl in my algebra class told me I had bedroom eyes. I told her she had bathroom lips and that was the end of that. But I looked in the mirror when I got home to see if I could tell what my eyes really looked like: dark and thick, like no place you'd want to go swimming.

The woman at the cash register was really giving me an evil look. Twenty after eleven. I leaned against the wall and sank to the floor where I couldn't see her, picking up a copy of a nearby zine on my descent so I could pretend I was

reading it if she walked over to check on me. It was called *No Regrets* and the cover was bright red with black ink. Dumb title. Everybody had regrets, even if they didn't want to talk about them. It looked like it might be funny, though. I read some of the poems in the front—they were short and silly. There was one about eating asparagus and how your pee smells weird afterward, which I really enjoyed because I always notice the same thing, but I never heard anybody mention it before.

A stack of zines hit the floor right next to where I was sitting. I sort of glanced in that direction, then zeroed in. *Escape Velocity*. That must be *her*!

"Sorry," she said loudly. "Did I bump you?"

She was speaking to me. "Uh, no." Not at all what I'd expected. Small, tiny almost, though her voice was big. She wore those fat, black boots girls seemed to like so much, but even wearing those her feet looked about a third the size of mine. She had on black jeans and a black leather jacket, and her hair was black too, about shoulder length with spikey ends that looked like they'd cut into her flesh if she took her protective coat off. I was so sure she'd be big—that was the way I'd been thinking about her—imposing, sort of, even scary.

I guess I must have laughed or snorted or something. I was just surprised. She spun around and glared at me.

"What's your problem?" Her voice was just like her haircut, sharp and dangerous. Big or little, she *was* kind of scary.

"No problem," I said. I put my hands up to show her I wasn't armed. "Are you Marisol? Who writes *Escape Velocity*?"

She slanted her head sideways so she was glaring at me cockeyed. "Yeah, so what if I am?"

"Nothing. I mean, I came here today to get the new issue. And to meet you."

She turned and faced me, hands on her hips. She reminded me of a little bitty Clint Eastwood or something. "How did you know I was coming today?"

"It says so in the zine. Number two will be available on March second, which is today." I was beginning to feel stupid looking up at her from the floor, so I slid back up the wall until I was towering over her, even though I'm only five foot ten. She backed up.

"So, is Marisol your real name, or a nom de plume? You know, a name you use..."

"I know what a nom de plume is. I'm not an idiot."

I didn't seem to be coming off too well. "So, it's your name then?"

"What are you, the FBI? Yeah, it's my name, all right?" She hiked her black backpack up on one shoulder and turned to go.

"So..." I didn't know what else to say. Here was the person who wrote all that great stuff in *Escape Velocity* and I wasn't saying the right things to get her to stick around. "Aren't you going to take copies of any of the other zines?"

She shrugged. "I have subscriptions to the ones I like. If I read all this stuff, I wouldn't have time to do my own writing."

I gave up on subtlety and held out a copy of *Bananafish*. "You might like this one."

Marisol rolled her eyes and fingered the magazine away from me like she didn't want to get her hands dirty. She flipped through the first few pages.

"It's mine," I said.

"No kidding. What a shock." She kept reading, though.

"Take it home, why don't you? It's free."

"Such a deal." She flipped back to the cover. "So, Giovanni. Is that your nom de plume?"

She was like a grenade that was about to go off in my hand. How the hell could I tell her my name was John? Nobody was named John anymore—it was a 1950s name. A name for your annoying uncle.

"My family's Italian," I said, skirting the issue. Not a *total* lie. Galardi is Italian, after all, even though we're about six generations removed from the hills of Tuscany.

"Yeah? Well, I'm a Puerto Rican Cuban Yankee lesbian, so that puts me a lot higher on the exotic scale than you, Giovanni Italian." She gave me a wallop on the arm with my own zine. "So, I'll take this home and look it over."

This time she did turn and leave, quickly, slipping through the revolving doors without even touching them.

I grabbed a copy of *Escape Velocity* #2 in the hand that still held *No Regrets* and raced out the door. She was already half a block down Newbury Street.

"Wait a minute!" I called out, jogging after her. "How about—do you want to go get an ice cream or something? And talk?"

Marisol turned around. "*Ice cream?* It's freezing out here! What are you, trying to pick me up? I told you I'm a lesbian."

"Absolutely not," I told her, just a little offended. "I'm not interested in that. I mean, it's better that you're a lesbian. I don't really like girls much." I knew I'd screwed myself the minute it came out. Her arms plowed into her waistline.

"For your information, dickhead, lesbians *are* girls. Don't they teach sex ed in your school system?"

"That's not...I said it wrong because you're making me nervous. I feel like I have to say everything fast or you'll run away."

She glared at me another few seconds and then her lip twisted up a little, like it might be considering smiling. "Okay. I'm not running. Slow down and say it right."

I started over, slowly. "I mean, I'm not looking for a girlfriend. I just want to talk to you. About writing. About your zine. We could get coffee if you don't want ice cream." I hated coffee, but it seemed like the kind of thing a Puerto Rican Cuban Yankee lesbian writer would order at eleven o'clock in the morning.

Marisol shrugged again. "Well, I got a little time, I guess. As long as you're not some crazy person who thinks he could turn me straight."

"No, really," I assured her. "I'm not crazy. I'm not a rapist. I'm not anything really."

Then she gave me this sort of half smile, one side of her mouth working only, and pointed her finger at my chest. "Actually, I suspect you are pretty damn crazy, Gio, but probably not dangerous crazy. Come on, I know a place."

I felt as if I'd been released from a trap, a little shaky and kind of scraped up, but really thankful. I wasn't John

anymore. I was Gio. And I was probably pretty damn crazy.

"You spent half the morning in Tower Records and you didn't get a copy of *Factsheet 5*?" Marisol said, banging her coffee cup down onto its saucer. She was almost through with her refill while I played with my original cup, now stone cold and way too milky. It was a cool place she'd taken me to, a bookstore café where you could read the shelves from your tiny table. We'd spent an hour discussing the technical aspects of zine production. She knew so much I started writing things down.

"I never heard of *Factsheet 5*," I said. "It's a zine?"

"No, no. It's not a freebie. You get it inside on the magazine racks. You actually have to spend a few bucks, but let me tell you, if you plan to keep making zines, you *have* to get a *Factsheet 5*."

"How come?"

Marisol leaned back in her chair and laid one heavy-booted foot on top of the other knee. It seemed so amazing to me that I was sitting in the Trident Bookstore Café on Newbury Street talking to this unusual person—at least I'd never met anybody like her—and having this great, weird time. I even liked the people at the other tables. There were two women with long gray hair, older than my mother probably, wearing long Indian skirts and hiking boots, discussing their acupuncturists. And at another table a group of college students, their clothes spattered with paint, argued about which galleries showed the most innovative work and which brand of veggie-burgers was the tastiest. (Toto, we're not in Darlington anymore.)

"It's a damn good thing you met me, Giovanni Italian. You don't know squat about the zine business," Marisol continued.

I took another sip of my chilly brew. God, you can feel the stuff eating away at your stomach. "I don't really think of it as a business. I just like writing, and I thought it would be fun to make a zine. I'm not trying to get rich on it or anything."

"Well, that's good, because you won't. None of us will. On the other hand, the closer you can come to breaking even on it, the more zines you'll be able to produce, right?"

"It didn't cost me that much. Just the copying and the cover stock."

"It adds up. Listen, *Factsheet 5* tells you how to do stuff cheaply, how to get a subscription list started, and the best thing is they review all the zines that are sent to them, which means people will write to you from all over the country and ask you to send them a copy of *Bananafish*. You wouldn't like that? Go back to Tower and get an *F5* and send a copy of your zine there right away." She was so serious about the whole thing.

"Well, okay, but really it's not that big a deal for me. I mean, it's not like what I have to say is going to change the world."

Marisol sat up straight and her face got tight. "So why bother then, if it's just some half-assed way to waste your time? If you're not committed to having people read what you've written? What have we been talking about all morning?"

"It's not half-assed..."

"Because I really hate that...people who don't take things seriously, who think everything is a big joke."

"It's not a joke. I worked hard on it."

But she wasn't even listening anymore. She was on a crusade or something. "It's a lie, you know, to pretend that nothing is important to you. It's hiding. Believe me, I know, because I hid for a long time. But now I won't do it anymore. The truth is bioluminescent. I don't lie, and I don't waste time on people who do." She pulled her backpack off the floor and started rummaging around in it for money to pay the bill.

"Wait a minute. Who says I tell lies?"

She looked me straight in the eye. "Tell me you don't."

Jesus. "Well, I can't say I *never* lie. I mean I don't always tell my parents the whole truth, but nobody does that. I don't lie to my *friends*." As I said it I was actually picturing this large group of people to whom I am forever honest and loyal, instead of lonely old Brian, to whom I'll say almost anything. Even my imagination lies.

She was counting out dollar bills now, so I reached in my pocket for a few of my own. "Do you know what 'coming out' really means?" she asked, looking me square in the face again. "It means you stop lying. You tell the truth even if it's painful, especially if it's painful. To everybody, your parents included."

"I'm not gay," I told her, though I really had no strong evidence for saying so. "At least I don't think I am."

"There are other closets."

"Actually, I suppose I *could* be gay." I was getting into the spirit of this truth-telling.

"Let me know when you decide."

"Anyway, I'm not lying in my zine, and I'm not lying to you." Much.

"You better not lie to me, Gio."

Gio. Well, that wasn't really fair. I mean, it was an innocent lie, and I'd told it before I knew she was such a truth zealot. It didn't seem like a good time to fess up, though.

"I'm not. I wouldn't," I said. I scanned the nearby shelves quickly and lucked out. The perfect thing. I grabbed a copy of *Nine Stories*, by J.D. Salinger, and slapped it down on the table, put my left hand on top of it and raised my right palm in the air. "I swear on my bible," I said as seriously as possible.

I guess Marisol appreciated luck too. She laughed. Not a big belly laugh, of course. Just a small explosion of air, but a definite yielding to mirth.

"You think you're pretty smart, Mr. Bananafish," she said.

"You know the book?" I asked.

"Of course I know the book. The best story is "Just Before...""

"Just Before the War with the Eskimos!" I yelled. "I knew you were going to say that!"

"You did not," she said, and slapped her money on the table. "You're funny, though. I appreciate that."

She stood up and tried to disappear into thin air again,

but I followed her out the door. "I'm here every week. At my dad's place on Marlborough Street. I never have anything to do, so maybe we could—"

"As long as you're alive, there's always plenty to do. You know John Berryman, the poet? He says people who are bored have no inner resources. Check it out: "Dream Song #14." Meet me here at eleven next Saturday morning. With a copy of *Factsheet 5*."

I watched her walk away down Newbury Street for just a minute (wondering what the hell a dream song was), but I had the feeling she wouldn't want me watching her, so I turned around and headed back to Tower Records. I was alive; there was plenty to do.

Chapter Three

It just wasn't funny. The idea was good: *Memoirs from Hell*. Things like where you slept (in dormitories where everybody else snored), who you had to sit next to at meals (people with runny noses and hacking coughs), what you had for breakfast every morning (liverwurst with aerosol cheese sprayed on top), where you shopped (only in warehouse superstores), the only recreational item you were allowed to own (a Barbie doll), the only book you were allowed to read (*Paradise Lost*). Stuff like that. Only it wasn't really working. They were giggles, but they weren't hitting home. They weren't deeply, evilly funny. I was just about to give up and peruse the book of John Berryman poems I got from the school library when Mom called upstairs.

"Johnny. Guess who I picked up on my way home from school?"

Damn it. Your best friend in hell (a dork nobody else notices who depends on you for the entirety of his social interaction).

"Come down and have a snack with Brian. He's hungry."

That was code for: Come down here and fix Brian something to eat because after teaching fifth graders all day I'm too tired to wait on your friends.

"Just a sec," I called back. I stuck *Memoirs from Hell* into the computer's memory, the better to remove it from mine. Maybe later it would work.

"Where'd you disappear after school?" Brian demanded to know as I came down the stairs.

"I wanted to get home. I didn't see you. I'm working on something."

"I told you to meet me at the Drama Club bulletin board. They put the cast list up!"

"Oh, right. Sorry. I forgot." He wasn't too offended to follow me into the kitchen. Mom was in there washing out her coffee thermos.

"I'm afraid there isn't lots to eat. Some cheese and crackers, maybe. A few bananas. I need to go to the store." Mom was never very big on "Hi, how are you? Did you have a good day?"

"That's okay, we'll find something, Mrs. Galardi. I mean, Mrs....Ms. Van Esterhower...howsen...Van Esterhausen." Mom's taking her maiden name back had really thrown old Brian for a loop. I couldn't say I was too thrilled by it either. It was weird to have to go to the high school office and change her name on all my records, like saying somebody else was my mother now, somebody whose name I barely knew how to spell.

"I know it's a mouthful. Why don't you just call me Anne, Brian? After all, you boys aren't children anymore." For some reason, I didn't like her announcing that to us; I mean, it seemed like the kind of thing I ought to tell *her*. *We're not children anymore, Mother!* She stuck the thermos in the dish drainer and gave us a little smile, but you could tell it was really costing her. "I'm going to disappear upstairs and take a little rest before I fix dinner. Would you answer the phone if it rings, Johnny?"

"Sure." She had to pass close to where I was standing to get through the doorway, but I knew she wouldn't touch me, and she didn't. I hadn't thought about it much lately, but for a while when I first noticed that Mom didn't touch me anymore, back around the time of the divorce I guess, it really bothered me. I thought about it all the time. True, she was never one of those kissy-type mothers, but as a little kid I'd curl up next to her on the couch in the evenings. Or,

you know, sit on her lap. And she was always pretty free with her hugs, so when it stopped all of a sudden—I was probably nine or ten—you can be sure I noticed it.

I'd go out of my way to stand where she'd be almost forced to bump into me, but she never did. She'd go out of *her* way to avoid it, or she'd wait me out, or she'd just plain ask me to get out of her way. I couldn't bring myself to say anything about it, so I'd just move. What were you supposed to say anyway? *Hey, Mom, am I disgusting? Am I diseased? How come all of a sudden you can't stand to touch me?* Anyway, it's something I've gotten used to. Now when I see Brian's mother kiss him or even pat his arm or something, it kind of gives me chills.

I pulled a hunk of Swiss cheese out of the refrigerator.

"Aren't you even going to ask me whether I got a part?"

"A part of what?"

"God," Brian exploded, "you are about the worst friend!"

He was probably right about that. "Oh, yeah, I forgot. The play. So, did you?"

Brian grabbed the cheese out of my hand and dumped it on the table. It was obvious he was dying to tell me, but now I'd kind of ruined it for him. I forced myself. "Well, did you or not? I'm asking you."

"Of course I did. They were desperate for boys," he said gloomily. "And I'm not Nazi Soldier Number Six. I'm the butler."

"Sounds good. What does the butler do?" I stuck a breadboard under the cheese and handed Brian a knife,

then found some crackers and rummaged in the fridge for something to drink. Not much. Enough orange juice to stretch with fizzy water.

"I'm in two scenes, and I have four lines. I mostly take people's coats on and off."

"Great! So you got in it! Is what's-her-name in it?" My good nature is severely limited, I know.

"*Violet*, for God's sake. Of course she's in it. She's *Maria*." He slid the knife through his thumb and the cheese simultaneously. The cheese pinked up before I could pull it out of the way. Brian started whirling around in a circle holding his injured digit up in the air with his other hand.

"Jesus! Stick it under the water!" I yelled. I never know what to do in an emergency, but I like to give the impression I'm in complete control. "All you have to do is say that girl's name and you're a bumbling nitwit," I complained.

"Ow, ow, ow," Brian sang as the water cleaned out the cut and bloodied the sink. Finally he held it up at eye level to inspect the damage.

"It's not that deep," I decided, based on nothing. I took out the Band-Aid box Mom kept above the stove.

"Like you would know," Brian said, self-pity thickening his voice.

I peeled back the plastic and handed him a sticky beige strip. I certainly didn't intend to touch the wound myself.

While he wrapped himself up, I tried to fix the cheese, but it refused to come clean. I had to amputate.

"She's got a boyfriend," Brian told his thumb.

"What?"

"She's got a *boyfriend*," he repeated so I could hear too.

"Violet, you mean?"

"Who else would I mean?"

"Well, fine. I mean, is this a total shock to you? I thought she went with some guy all last year."

"I thought you hardly knew who she was." The guy was in a really pissy mood, you could tell.

"You talk about her all the time. It's hard to avoid a certain amount of knowledge!" I said.

Old Brian slumped back into a chair. "It's not like I expected a miracle to happen to me. It's just that I didn't expect a miracle to happen to Vincent Brazwell either."

"Vincent Brazwell? She's going with *him*?" This *was* a pathetic story.

"He got tall. And he *sings*."

"Who cares if he sings?"

"Obviously Violet cares. He's playing the male lead. The captain guy. They get to proclaim their love in front of the whole audience. In front of the stupid butler."

I took another look in the fridge. Too bad I couldn't let Brian have one of Mom's beers. She'd have a fit. But there wasn't much else I could do for the guy. I refilled his glass with orange-flavored water. Yum.

"Look, you've got to stop thinking about Violet Neville. She's not the only girl in the world."

"She's the only decent one in Darlington."

"I doubt that."

"Name me one other."

"Brian, I don't really pay any attention. I mean, Rapun-

zel could be sitting in front of me, and I probably wouldn't notice. Girls aren't my thing."

Brian shook his head. "You're so weird. No wonder you hang around with me."

"You're just figuring that out?"

He brightened. "I know! Next weekend let me go into Boston with you. I can look on Newbury Street!"

Whoa. Here was a real bad idea. "What's the use of that? Even if you see somebody, you'll never see her again. You're not going to pick up some babe in Boston and ship her out here to Darlington to go to the movies on Saturday night."

"But it makes me feel good to look at them. *Please!*"

Damn it. "The thing is...I can't, really."

"Why not? I haven't come in with you for months. Your dad doesn't care."

"Well, actually we've been sort of...doing things together. I mean, you know, spending more time...doing things." I swear to God I had the feeling Marisol was looking over my shoulder, listening to me lie.

"You and your dad? He's too busy to do things with you."

"Well, we're trying, you know. I just don't think right now is a good time for you to come. Maybe in a few weeks or something. I'll let you know."

Brian glared at his taped-up finger like it was a crystal ball. "Meanwhile I'm stuck here in hell. Where my only friend thinks my life is a big joke, and the girl of my dreams is in love with a tenor."

My eyebrows peaked. Not bad, Brian, old man. Not bad at all.

Friday night: Bertucci's again. If I get my choice, which I usually do, I always choose Bertucci's. Best pizza, in my opinion. Dad always orders some pasta dish. (Did you ever notice there's no such thing as "spaghetti" anymore? It's all "pasta" now, or some fancy Italian name that ends in *chini* or *tini* or *lini*.) Pizza is way too juvenile for a guy like Dad. What if he was chowing down on a big tomatoey triangle and there were stringy mozzarella hammocks swinging in the breeze when one of those famous authors he publishes came walking over to him? Famous authors, I imagine, don't eat pizza either, at least not in public. Only takeout. Poor schmucks.

I couldn't figure out why Dad kept clearing his throat. He wasn't even eating the tortellini, just picking out the little broccoli trees. Then finally he got around to his subject.

"So I ran into Peter Otto the other day!" Hearty smile.

"Who?"

"Peter Otto. They used to come to dinner once in a while. Your mother works with his wife, Jane. Jane Otto. They have a little girl...."

"Yeah. I remember." Vaguely. Little girl wouldn't stay home with a baby-sitter. I had to watch television with her to keep her out of the grown-ups' hair. I think I made her cry.

"...Bitsy or Pinky or some such name."

"Uh-huh."

"Anyway, Mr. Otto told me your mother is thinking of...probably will be...getting married again." A look of gravity came onto his face, just in case I hadn't been aware that we were now discussing something *important*.

I thought it over while I teased a big wad of caramelized onions off a cheesy slice and stuck it into my mouth. Wouldn't Mom be pleased to know her personal business had been discussed by her ex-husband and some guy she once made a pork roast for? Probably over a pale ale at some brew pub or something. The news interspersed with a few slightly nasty, man-to-man type jokes.

"I assume she's discussed this with you, John."

"None of my business, really," I said, freeing another slice from its brethren.

"Well, it's certainly of *interest* to you. I mean, you've *met* the man, I take it?"

"I know him," I admitted.

"And do you approve of him? Does he seem...appropriate?"

What the hell was he talking about? This was putting a crimp in my chewing. "What do you care? You're not *her* father."

"John, I'm trying to speak to you man-to-man here. I thought you were old enough to engage in this conversation. But if it's too painful for you..."

It was like a great energy, the anger that blew up out of my chest and exploded from my mouth. I hadn't seen it coming, didn't even know it was in there. "Old enough?" I screamed so loud he dropped a forkful of vegetables and

a little piece of tomato splatted on his tie. "Since when did it matter how old I was? You expected me to understand you when I was ten years old! One minute you were bossing me around like your miniature slave, and the next minute you wanted to dish the dirt with me, discuss your manly problems, how my mother had let you down. I was ten! I don't think I was *quite* old enough to listen to that bullshit."

I hadn't let him get to me that way in years. I tried to cool down. What the hell did I care about any of them? It was ancient history. But I couldn't seem to cap the geyser. "It's not the least bit painful for me to see my mother finally act a little bit happy, after watching her sit around in the dark for five years. I don't care who the hell she marries. So what if I'm not in love with the guy? Her taste in husbands never was too terrific."

That felt so good. I've been places before when somebody's throwing a tantrum and you feel like you shouldn't stare at them, like they're embarrassed enough already that they blew up in public. But I wasn't embarrassed at all. I was glad there was a roomful of people there to sneak peeks at my father, whose blotchy face was surely an admission of guilt.

He was a pro though. Probably he'd had a few temperamental writers holler at him in public before. He motioned to the waiter, who came hopping over like the White Rabbit. Signed the credit card slip and got the food in take-out boxes before you could say "public humiliation."

I walked ahead of him the six blocks back to his place

on Marlborough Street, but I had to wait for him at the door because I'd left my key inside.

Without looking at me, he clicked open the door. "I'm going out," he said, handing me the greasy boxes. "I'll be late."

"Thank you," was the only response I could come up with.

Chapter Four

Dad usually slept late on Saturday mornings, but just in case he decided to get up to deliver a comeback to my Bertucci's outburst, I figured I ought to disappear as early as possible. Since I had several hours to kill before I had to meet Marisol, I took along the second issue of *Escape Velocity*, which I'd already read several times, and the copy of *No Regrets* I'd picked up last Saturday and skimmed while waiting at Tower Records. And of course the copy of *Factsheet 5* I'd gone back for at Marisol's insistence. (I'd read it already, picked up a few tips, and sent a copy of *Bananafish* to the reviewer, but in case I needed brownie points with Marisol, I could always pull it out to show how obedient I am.) These, a notebook and pen, and Berryman's *77 Dream Songs* I put into a small backpack, planning to stay gone as long as possible.

There was a bagel place a few blocks away from Dad's town house, usually full of Emerson College students displaying multitudinous piercings and tattoos, but it was relatively empty at 8:30 on a Saturday morning. I figured they wouldn't mind if I sat in a corner for a couple of hours as long as I nibbled an onion bagel and nursed a cup of tea. The first thing I did was reread Marisol's best new piece.

E S C A P E

I suppose there are people who grow
up with no wish to escape, but they
aren't people I know. Is this a
legacy passed on to me by my
father, an escapee from Cuba who's
now thoroughly entangled in the
kudzu of American life? Or from my
white mother, who felt she had to rip herself
away from her aristocratic background and
marry a refugee with an accent in order to
be taken seriously as a social worker for
the needy poor, but who now counsels mostly
the needy rich in her carpeted offices in
Cambridge? Or does it come from my birth
parents, about whom I know only that they
were Puerto Rican, and that they escaped
from me?

And now I have to run too. To escape from them, of course, as all children have to do, to escape from their understanding, their always tolerant love. I have to test myself against the world without the buffer, and I have to give them a break from dealing with their outlandish lesbian daughter. When I opened the closet door my mother assured me I could always count on her support, but she cried for days with the bathroom door locked. She was mourning expectations, I think: dresses and a wedding, boyfriends and babies, things she was looking forward to. (One of those things even I had been looking forward to. I still am.)

My father didn't say anything to me for several days, but I heard the two of them talking at night in their bedroom. She was trying to convince him that it would be all right, that it was not perverse, that I was still their beloved child. It's been more than a year now, and my father has never discussed my lesbianism with me, but he speaks to me again and pretends nothing has changed.

My mother, within a week, had joined PFLAG (Parents and Friends of Lesbians and Gays) and announced to me that the two of us would march together in the Gay Pride parade. I know this makes me lucky. I know there are parents who would rage and scream and throw their children out of the house after an admission like mine. And still I resent them. One denies and one embraces. My father wears a blindfold, and my mother wants to out-gay me! I barely know what it means to be homosexual myself, and she's racing ahead of me, reading all the literature, consulting experts, wanting to "explore my feelings." I don't want to explore lesbianism with my mother, at least not now.

I need to figure out what it all means by myself. I need to have a world that is not open to my mother. I need to cross barriers by myself, not holding her hand. I am not her baby anymore. I am not her best friend. I want to be her daughter, but later, after I've figured out who Marisol is by herself. After I've escaped.

I kept thinking, how could anybody know so much about themselves? And about their parents! (And I wondered which of those four things she was still looking forward to.)

Not that I don't think about things, but I don't usually end up coming to any conclusions—I just get frustrated that everything seems so complicated: my mother's depression, my father's swinging-bachelor lifestyle, my own stalled life, stuck in neutral while everybody else my age is accelerating like mad.

I wondered what *my* mother's reaction would be if I announced I was gay. I could imagine: She'd give a little snort through her nose and say, "Just my luck. I should have known something else would go wrong." Then she'd turn out the living room lights for a few more years.

Dad would probably swallow his bite of broccoli and say calmly, "When you're older, John, we'll engage in this conversation again. Man-to-man. It's of no interest to me now."

I got out my notebook and started to write a little bit about escape too, sort of an answer to Marisol's article.

How long would it take my parents to notice if I escaped? It's possible they never would. Mom would be happy I'm staying in my room, periodically calling up the stairs to tell me she'd left a few bananas in the kitchen for me, some cheese. Or she'd decide I was eating out somewhere, which was fine as long as I hadn't taken the car. She likes the car to stay home, just in case she wants to drive it herself and have that accident she's always waiting for.

When Dad showed up Friday after work Mom would shout through the keyhole, "Go home. He wants to be alone!" Happy that I'd come over to her side at last. (The lonesome crackpot side.) Dad himself would be delirious with joy. No more slogging through Friday night dinners with Junior. No more hiding the babe parade. No more public humiliation. Hallelujah!

Somehow writing this was getting me down. I couldn't wait until it was time to go see Marisol, but there was a good half hour before she'd be there, so I picked up the Berryman book and turned to the poems Marisol had quoted from last week. Most of the poems went right past me; I felt like I couldn't get a starting point with them, though the language was so strange I kind of liked being inside their world.

"Dream Song #14" cracked me up. This guy was definitely cool, talking about how life was boring, but you weren't supposed to admit it. The funny thing was, the part Marisol liked about having inner resources was something the guy's *mother* kept telling him over and over, which he obviously ignored. I mean, I guess everybody just hears poetry the way they want to, the way it fits them the best.

With twenty minutes still to kill, I started thumbing through *No Regrets* again, past the poetry in the front to a kind of stream-of-consciousness autobiography piece in the back. The type was surrounded by tiny hand-drawn stars and moons and musical notes and teddy bears and arrows, all kinds of things raining down like confetti around the words.

At the bottom of the page was a thick tree trunk that branched out around the last sentences so that the leaves puffed through the article too, like clouds.

Just so you know my name Diana Tree is my real name but not the name I was born with which is Diana Crabtree which is not the sort of name I want to have and I don't see why we can't just pick our own names the Diana part is all right I can live with it it means huntress and it's a strong woman's kind of name but no way on the Crab part because that is just the opposite of everything I believe in which is that we need to be open to new experiences not complain about things or look for the bad side so I've cut out the Crab part and that's not me anymore only the Tree part is me a good part of me a tall and wavy and always growing part of me which reflects the real person inside me and not just a patriarchal handle that relates me to lots of dead persons who probably wouldn't like me anyway.

When you live on Cape Cod like I do
the natural elements like trees and
sand and wind and water become
important to you they become almost
the most important things they help
you to forgive people for hurting you
because you realize that people
including yourself can never be as
trustworthy as nature because people
don't live long enough they don't
understand how much they need each
other except maybe for those people
who have been on earth before and have
some little memory of it and maybe I
am one of those people because I truly
want to be trustworthy and hurt no one
if only I could live longer than
eighty or ninety years but anyway I
feel it can only help me to jettison
my Crab and become a Tree with roots
holding me deeply to earth and
branches shading all those close to me
don't be afraid to come under.

I'd never read anything written like that before, all piled together, and it was sort of fun to figure it out. But this Diana was a tad odd. Maybe she'd been on earth before? What was that, Buddhist or something? New Age or just old hippie? I had to admit I liked the stuff about taking the part of her name that worked for her and cutting off the rest. That was sort of what I'd done too, wasn't it? Not really a *lie*, just rearranging the truth a little bit. Of course Diana had come right out and admitted it.

When I looked at my watch it was almost eleven! Damn, I'd gotten so wrapped up reading *No Regrets* I hadn't kept track of the time. I only had half a dozen blocks to cover, but I sprinted the first few anyway, then slowed down so I wouldn't get there out of breath and sweaty. It was warm for the second week of March, and I'd worn my winter coat.

I could see her from a block away standing in front of the Trident, all in black again. She seemed to be talking to the blond guy standing next to her, some muscley dude who was wearing a tight T-shirt, as if his protruding biceps couldn't bear to be restricted by long sleeves. I could just imagine how thrilled Marisol was that *he'd* stopped to chat.

But as I got closer I could see they were laughing; Marisol had her hand resting on one of those iron arms.

"Gio!" she called when she saw me. "There you are! Birdie and I got here early and got coffee to take out. It's so nice I thought we could walk down and sit in the park."

"Sure." Birdie? More like Hawk, I would have said. His long nose pointed to a very toothy smile.

"So, you're *Gio*. I'm Birdie Gates, Marisol's most *trusted* confidante," the blond chirped at me, and I realized my initial assumption about those muscles was wrong. Birdie's speech was quite precise, almost prissy, and he inflected certain words with an odd emphasis as if he wanted to make sure I knew he was gay.

"I didn't think you'd mind if Birdie came along. He was at loose ends. Dumped by his latest beau," Marisol explained.

"Dumped? I dumped *his* sorry butt, if you please."

Marisol handed me a large styrofoam cup as we started down Newbury Street toward the public garden. I'd never be able to drink that much. "Did you put cream in it?" I asked.

"I put half a cow in just like you did last week." She reached in her jacket pocket. "I brought sugar too. It didn't seem like unadulterated brew was your specialty."

I took the little white packages and stuffed them in my pocket. "Thanks. Maybe next week it'll be warm enough for ice cream."

"*Next* week?" Birdie shrieked. "What, do you two have a regular *appointment* or something?"

"I just meant, next time, whenever that might—"

Marisol interrupted me. "He's just jealous. I told you, Birdie, Gio is a writer. I need to talk to other writers sometimes. We'll find you another boyfriend, and you won't want to spend all your Saturdays with me."

Birdie looked grumpy. "Well, it won't be *him*," he said, thrusting his head in my direction.

Marisol glanced at me. "You're sure? Already?"

"He's not *gay*! It doesn't take a *Ph.D.* to figure it out."

"Am I missing something?" I inquired.

"Well, you said you didn't like girls, and you didn't seem too sure about being straight. I figured Birdie would know..."

"I always know," Birdie assured me. "I can always tell right away."

"And then if you *were* gay...since Birdie's between guys..."

"You were fixing me up?" I was amazed.

Marisol shrugged. "Not necessarily. I was just seeing what would happen. It didn't seem so unlikely. Since I like you both."

She said it very offhandedly like that. "Since I like you (both)." Honest to God a shiver ran through my body. A big one. Like an earthquake tremor. Nobody ever said they liked me. Ever. Not even Brian, who probably actually doesn't.

"Well, *ix-nay* on the fix-up. He's *not*. The way he walks. And talks. And laughs..." Birdie was explaining to Marisol.

"Come on. You're stereotyping! I can't believe you!"

"*Sweet*heart, it's not stereotyping when *I* do it. I read the subtleties. And besides, I can tell by the way he *looks* at you."

I stopped in my tracks. Well, that ought to send Marisol running. "What do you mean? I'm not even sure myself if I'm gay or not. I mean, I've been thinking maybe I am."

"You *have*? Are you attracted to *men*?" Birdie asked.

"Well, no. But I'm not attracted to women either."

"Oh, *well*, that's just dysfunctional, not *gay*," Birdie announced confidently. I was lost for a comeback.

The park was practically empty, only a few early lunchers perched on benches near the path, a couple of twelve-year-olds on roller blades racing for the bridge. "Down by the pond. In the sun," Marisol directed, and Birdie and I followed her. We settled ourselves on the edge of the empty pool and opened our steaming cups.

"Are you disappointed?" Marisol asked me.

"Disappointed?"

"Not to be gay?"

I shrugged. "It's just Birdie's opinion. Besides, I don't get disappointed. I don't feel emotions like that."

"What a crock!" Birdie said.

Marisol gave me that lopsided grin. "I've been there. It's self-protective. But it's no good for you in the long run."

"John Berryman says life is boring," I said. I guess I thought Marisol would be proud of me for going out and finding the poem, or something, for being so cool. Instead, she turned on me.

"For God's sake, Gio, don't emulate *Berryman*. The poems are wonderful, of course, but the guy killed himself. His mother was right; his sensibility led him to a high bridge."

I didn't know what to say, but I didn't want to seem too surprised by the news. "Great artists often live on the edge," I said, my voice tinged, I thought, with mystery.

Birdie leaned across Marisol and laid a thick fist over one of my wrists. "Well, *pardon* my bluntness, Gio, but you

are so self-consciously odd, I just *have* to ask: What the fuck is *up* with you?"

Marisol had been taking a big slurp from her cup and she almost choked, spilling blistering coffee all over my leg. "Birdie! For God's sake! You know how I feel about that word!"

"I'm sorry, I'm sorry. It slipped out. I forgot." He withdrew his hand.

"You promised me you wouldn't use it!"

"I know! I'm sorry! What else can I say? Mea culpa, for God's sake."

"What word?" I asked, brushing liquid off my clothes.

"The F word," Marisol said.

"The F word? Everybody says that."

"Well, I don't. And you better not say it around me either. It's not just a swear word; it's a hateful word. It's a violent word. It's not about sex or love or anything like that. It's ugly. It just means I want to hurt you."

"It's been stricken from my vocabulary," I assured her.

"Oh, yeah, he kisses up now that I've made one little mistake," Birdie complained.

"One?" Marisol said. "That'll be the day. Going off on somebody like that..." Suddenly her face got very flat and pale. She was looking over my shoulder. "Jesus!"

"What's wrong?" I turned to see what she was looking at. A large, bouncy woman in slacks and thick sneakers was waving at us as she came down the path. Her short, straight hair flapped happily around her cheeks.

"Oh, look!" Birdie said. "Here comes Dorothy *Hamill*; she must have *skated* here from *Oz*!"

"I can't believe it. She followed me." Marisol shook her head.

"*Helen!*" Birdie exclaimed as the woman closed in. "It's so *nice* to see you again. It's been...*hours!*"

"Mother, what are you doing here?" Marisol asked.

"Nothing, sweetie. I was planning to look into a few shops, Laura Ashley and such, and I just happened to see you sitting here with your friends...."

She glanced hopefully in my direction. "You must be Gio."

"Yes, ma'am. Nice to meet you." I stuck out my hand, then retracted it and stood up first, then stuck it out again. It was a graceless performance.

"The pleasure is mine," she assured me. "Are you from the North End? Not that I think all the Italians in Boston live in the North End, but it is such a wonderful *community*."

"No, I'm from Darlington. Up on the North Shore."

"Oh, what a lovely spot! How lucky you are!"

"Yes, ma'am." Lovely my ass. I was having a hard time believing this big lady with the gray face and wide pants was Marisol's mother. Of course she hadn't borne her, but still, it was incongruous to imagine the two of them living in the same house, eating the same food, putting their laundry in the same washing machine. I mean, this woman looked like Eleanor Roosevelt, if only Eleanor had had the fashion sense to chop her hair off in a straight line from one earlobe to the other.

"Okay. You've done your research. Better get on to Laura's now," Marisol said, not unkindly.

"Well, I'm so glad I saw you sitting here."

"Mmm. What a happy accident."

"Have a lovely day, dear." Mrs. Guzman looked over her shoulder twice as she retracted her steps up the path and waved each time.

"What a *hoot*!" Birdie said, laughing. "She's a stitch!"

"You don't think it was a coincidence she showed up here?" I asked.

"My mother leaves nothing to chance."

Birdie lay back on the ground to rest from his hysteria. "Helen came for the same reason *I* did, only her hopes were rather *skewed* in the other *direction*."

"Hope springs eternal," Marisol said. "She was hoping to find that you were straight."

I snickered. "Let me know what she thinks. Maybe we ought to take a poll. I could decide my sexuality based on the conclusions of a survey."

But Marisol wasn't laughing with me. "Don't you care, one way or the other?"

"Not particularly."

But my smile got shaky when Marisol stared at me, her dark eyes snagging mine like a fish hook. "Well, you *should*," she commanded. "If *you* don't know who you are, how is anybody else supposed to get to know you?"

When she put it like that, it was something to think about.

"That's assuming anyone else wants to *bother*," Birdie added cheerfully.

Chapter Five

"You walking home?" I called over to Brian. He was fumbling around in his locker, trying to extricate his jacket from under a pile of books. Papers snowed out around him and fell on his shoes. I'd bet you at least half of those papers had "Organization!" written across the top in red ink.

"Yeah, but I've got rehearsal first."

"Again?"

"That's the way you do a play. You rehearse every day."

He was an expert on drama now. "Not on the weekends," I pointed out.

"Well, of course, not on the weekends." He stuffed all the crap he didn't want back into the metal coffin and slammed the door.

"Fine," I said, but I was actually a little bit disappointed. I felt like talking for some reason. Marisol hadn't been able to meet me last weekend, and it was like I'd gotten used to having a conversation with somebody at least once a week. I missed it. Not that Brian had anything nearly as interesting to say as Marisol.

But it turned out he did have something kind of surprising to tell me. "Hey, John, you'll never guess what." He practically pinned me to my locker so he could whisper it without the whole hallway hearing him. "I met a girl!"

I pushed him back; he was making me claustrophobic. "What do you mean 'met'? You mean you *spoke* to one?"

"Yeah, a bunch of times. She's in the play. She's a freshman. She's a nun."

"You met a fourteen-year-old nun? She sounds perfect for you."

"Shh!" He glanced around for eavesdroppers. "In the play she's a nun," he whispered. "Her name's Emily Prine. Do you know her?"

"You know I don't know any girls. Not even Violet Weevil."

"Neville. Who, by the way, I'm losing interest in."

"Thank the Lord."

"Now that I'm getting to know her, she's kind of shallow." You could tell he was real proud of coming up with that insight.

"No kidding."

"I'm going to ask Emily to go out with me Saturday night. Today I'm going to ask her." He was cracking his knuckles so hard I was afraid he might accidentally definger himself.

"Did you bring your inhaler? Want me to wait around in case you need CPR?"

He gave me a shove. "Get out of here, Mr. Cool. You better find yourself a girl pretty soon."

"Why would I want to do that?"

"Because the Junior Prom is only a month away."

Of course, this warranted a laugh. "And you think I'm going to the Junior Prom?"

Brian shrugged. "Everybody goes to the prom. The whole class. It's fun. There's a dinner before and a break-fast afterward."

"I can probably rustle up my own grub for the evening, Bri. I don't think the *food* is supposed to be the highlight of the event."

"You jerk. I'm going. If Emily will go out with me this weekend, I'm going to ask her to the prom."

I looked at my watch. "Don't let me make you late for your butler rehearsal."

Old Bri shot me his meanest look—kind of like a frus-trated squirrel—and stomped off down the hall.

By the time I walked home I was feeling a little frus-trated myself. Edgy, at loose ends. It didn't help matters to be met at the door by my mother on her way out.

"I'm going to the store for shrimp. Al's coming for din-

ner, and I want it to be nice. We can all...talk about things. You know." Mom had finally given Al the go-ahead last week, and now they were constantly sitting around *planning* things.

"I'll just eat in my room."

"No! We want you to eat with us! Al does. So we can talk."

"Talk about what? The wedding?"

"Wedding? No, no. About the three of us. Afterward. You know, where we'll live and everything."

"Live? We're moving?" Somehow it hadn't occurred to me that this marriage was going to change *my* life very much. Now here she was talking about *moving*?

Mom sighed. "I want to get to the store, Johnny, so I can get back and make dinner. We'll discuss this later."

"Or not," I said, turning to climb the stairs. No way was I moving. Where to? That big old haunted house in Chesterfield where Al lived with his mother? Not likely.

Possibly Mom slammed the door a little harder than necessary.

I was sure when we exchanged phone numbers in the park I'd never call Marisol. I was glad to have the number—I'd even memorized it in about two seconds before folding the paper into my wallet—but I hated talking to people on the phone. Nobody ever sounded right when you couldn't see them, when you were connected by the magic of fiber optic cables. They either sounded fake happy, like they were so

excited you called, or else they grunted and grumbled as if they'd have to go get the Prozac if you intended to talk much longer. That's how my mother always sounded if I had to call her from Dad's house. She sounded the way a bassett hound looks.

But after an hour of staring out the window watching two little kids argue about the right way to hit a baseball (and kind of hoping they'd break a window or something testing their techniques), I was starting to lose it. I dialed the number without even looking at the paper.

"Lo!" came the familiar voice.

"Marisol?"

"Yup. Who's this?"

"Umm, Joh...Gio. It's Gio."

"Hey! Hi! Watcha doing?"

"Not much. Just trying to stay sane."

"Tell me about it. I have to go to some bullshit Gifted and Talented Awards dinner tonight with my parents. I was going to ditch it, but my mother found out about it from the mother of some other G and T bozo and now I have to show up." She sounded fine, just the way she did in the café or sitting in the park.

"I guess that means you're gifted and talented, huh?"

"Yeah, me and two-thirds of the graduating class. That's what the parents are paying for at a private school, you know. Rich people can't bear the idea that their kids are just ordinary. We're *all* gifted and talented."

"*You* probably really are, though."

"Of course I am. You need to ask?"

Something she'd said before had just registered. "You're graduating? You're a senior?"

"I am graduating and getting the hell out, Gio. Escaping!"

"Where to? You're going to college?"

"I guess so. It's the easiest way. My parents can't legitimately fight it. I applied all over the country, everywhere except New England. I'm hoping for Stanford. California seems just about far enough."

"Wow. I haven't even started thinking about college. I've got another year, though."

"Well, get on it, brother! If you sit on your thumbs, you'll end up at a state college or something. They'll want you to keep living at *home* or some damn thing. You better start making plans!"

I wasn't really in the mood for a lecture on life-planning, besides which it was one of my father's favorite topics. "Hey, Marisol, would you mind...could I read you something I started writing? I guess it's for the zine, but I'm kind of stuck on it. Maybe you can help me."

"Sure. I got a half hour before I have to polish up my brains and go show off for my parents's friends."

"Great." I picked quickly through my backpack and pulled out the notebook I'd been writing in at the bagel shop. I took a deep breath and read her the unfinished piece, the one about whether my parents would even notice if I escaped. I tried to make it sound humorous, but I could tell it wasn't coming off that way.

"Your parents are way different than mine," was Marisol's first comment.

"I guess."

"I know you were probably exaggerating..."

"A little. I mean, it's not like my mother just leaves a banana on the stairs and takes off. She's getting remarried. You know, there's lots on her mind."

"Uh-huh. And the part about your dad being so happy you're gone?"

Why had I read her this piece? It was nothing but depressing. And dumb. "That part is probably true. It doesn't work, does it? I mean, I wanted it to be funny, but..."

"No, Gio. Don't try to make it funny. Write the truth of it. It might turn out to be funny or it might not. Don't worry about that part. Just write it the way you're feeling it."

"I don't know. It's kind of a waste of time."

From downstairs I could hear Mom yelling. "Al's here! We're going to eat soon. Come down and say hello!"

"I'm on the phone!" I yelled back, covering the mouthpiece. "Hold on!" I was almost glad I had an excuse to hang up. Marisol was getting on a wrong track here. Sure, she wrote some serious pieces, but I did humor, not this soul-searching stuff.

"Listen, my mom's boyfriend is here. I've got to go have dinner with them. They're suddenly into us being a 'family' or something. It's creepy."

"Write it down, Gio. After dinner go to your room and write down what happened and how you feel about it. Your writing is good—it really is. Just don't run away from the feelings."

I had to laugh. "Who are you to tell me not to run away? You can't *wait* to escape."

There was no sound for a minute, and I was afraid I'd made her mad.

"Marisol?"

"I don't run away from myself, Gio. I don't lie," she said finally. Her voice sounded strained, as if she was talking while doing something very difficult, like balancing on a tightrope. "I have to leave to find out who I really am inside this person my parents have tried to manufacture. But I don't run from my feelings. Believe it or not, I love my parents. Sometimes it scares me to think about leaving them and going off by myself. What if I can't make it on my own?"

I was so surprised. "Of course you'll make it. If you can't, nobody can."

"That's what I'm afraid of. That nobody can. Not really."

"Oh, thanks. That's a comforting thought."

She sighed. "Yeah. Well, go eat with the boyfriend. I have to figure out how to dress in something that approaches normality so my mother won't be horrified in front of her cronies."

"Can you meet me Saturday? At eleven? Or earlier?"

Again there was a pause. "I don't know. I guess. Bring something to read me. What you write about dinner or something."

"Okay. You bring something too."

"It's so weird that we're, sort of, friends," she said. "But I guess stranger things have happened."

* * *

When you hear the word *fiancé*, you don't usually think of an old, bald guy, do you? To me the word ought to be reserved for young couples who are at least virgins at life if not in sexual experience. But that's what my mother's smiley, fifty-two-year-old boyfriend calls himself: "your mother's fiancé."

"Since I'm your mother's fiancé," he says to me, "I think we ought to get to know each other a little better." The littler the better is my opinion, but I keep it to myself. It's easier to just be busy when old Al shows up. This evening, however, is a command performance: a discussion of the postnuptial living arrangements.

Now, I know perfectly well where I plan to live, right here in the same house I've lived in for almost seventeen years, the house in which I have raised guppies and suicidal goldfish, the house whose gutters I clogged more than once with tennis balls, the house upon whose walls my fitful growth has been recorded, the house my father gave to my mother in the divorce settlement in which she lost her good humor.

Still, I go downstairs to eat with Al (knowing the only other option is starvation). He can hardly wait to give me the good news. Mom is still retrieving the final edibles from the kitchen when he tucks himself under the table and says, "I just want you to know that my home is plenty big enough for all of us."

Mom scurries back in. "Why don't we eat first before we discuss matters? That pasta will get cold."

I dump a load of shrimp and tomato sauce over my spaghetti, intending to obtain sustenance as quickly as possible in case I feel the need to throw a tantrum before too long and leave. "What home is that, Al?" I ask innocently.

"My place in Chesterfield. It's a big old place." Al is barely toying with his dinner, describing with one arm the expansiveness of his manse. "Of course, my mother has most of the first floor. It's her house, really, but she's no trouble at all. You'll like her," he assures me.

I'm *sure.*

I gesture toward my mother. "So, who'll be the lady of the house, then? My mother or yours?" A sweet smile.

"Oh, hell...heck, they get along like gangbusters, don't you, Annie?"

"Your mother is a dear," mine says tactfully. I have to wonder what the hell is in this marriage for her. Is it just redeeming some hurt pride or something? But then old Al leans over and rubs her shoulders real softly, and she smiles at him kind of shyly. God, don't tell me it's *sex.* I have to look away.

And so it begins. I have to tell them, "Look, I'm not moving anywhere. You two can feel free to go, but I'm staying right here. I have one year of school left, and I'm not starting all over at some new place. So get it out of your heads that Granny and I are going to be roomies." I can see where this is going so I shove in more food.

Al says he understands it's a little upsetting to me; Mom says the decision is not mine to make. I say, okay, move me, but I'm still going to school in Darlington.

"Do you know how much it costs to go to school in a town you don't live in?" Mom says. "And there aren't any buses that go directly. Chesterfield is only a half hour away—you can come back to see your friends whenever you want to." (What friends are those, I wonder?)

"I'll drive in then," I tell her. "I'll get a job and pay for the school myself. And drive here every day." I'm not even sure why I'm fighting so hard, because I don't like my school anyway. Nobody besides Brian would even know I left, and now that he's smitten with some freshman, he wouldn't care either. All I know is my mother marrying this bald guy is weird enough; I don't want anything else to change right now.

"Drive?" she screams. "It's too far!" After she just said it's "only" a half hour.

"Well, if I can't drive and there aren't any buses, how do you figure I'm going to come and visit all my dear old friends? This sucks, you know that? It really sucks!"

And finally the time has come to make a dramatic exit. I've eaten all the shrimp and most of the spaghetti anyway. It's time to retire to my room and allow them to reflect upon the damage they intend to do to mother's poor boy. I detour through the kitchen on my way to the stairs to grab an ice cream bar from the freezer. No reason to skip dessert.

It was funny enough. Smart. Nasty. I could show it to Marisol on Saturday. It was the part I didn't write down that bothered me, though. The part that happened later, when Mom came up to my room after Al left and sat on the very end of my bed, far away from where I was leaning against pillows, and blinked back half a teaspoon of moisture. She never cries, so this was a little unnerving.

"I don't want to hurt you, Johnny," she said, staring down at the old Indian print bedspread that used to be hers. "But I have to think of myself now. You're almost grown. Pretty soon you'll leave me too. And, God help me, I do love Al. So if he wants to live with his mother, then we will. Because I just couldn't bear to lose him now."

She was bawling over Goofy! I couldn't believe it! "You think Al's going to leave you because you won't share bed and board with his mother?"

"You may not understand this, John, but it was hard for me to let anybody get close, after so many years. Now that I've done it, I'm not taking any chances," she said.

"Jesus, don't you have any pride?" I said. That was really mean, I know. Like I said before, sometimes when I know what will hurt people, I can't stop myself from saying it. I've noticed, though, that I'm hardly the only person with this affliction. And at least I feel pretty crappy afterward.

She looked like she wanted to slap my face, but she didn't. Of course. That would mean touching me. Instead she just stood up and walked out.

I started thinking about what had happened at the table—Al leaning over and rubbing her shoulder. It wasn't whether or not they were having sex that was shocking. It was that *he* was allowed to *touch* her. He'd done it so casually, and she'd accepted it without a twinge—this had not been the first time. Did the guy even realize what that meant? He'd actually made contact! Broken through the invisible barrier. He was allowed to touch my mother, and *I wasn't!*

For some reason that hurt so damn much, I felt like crying myself. But, of course, I didn't. I probably don't even remember how.

Chapter Six

"I thought you might like to order in tonight, John. Maybe Chinese for a change."

I didn't know what was going on. Dad had been weird ever since he picked me up. We'd had the same Friday evening routine for a hundred years now: He pulls up in the Lexus, I'm waiting behind the door with my duffel bag, he honks, I sprint down the sidewalk and hop in the front seat. He doesn't even have to turn the motor off. He also doesn't have to talk to my mother, which is just fine with her too.

But today it was different. I was waiting as usual, the car pulled up, I sprinted, but he was out of the car by the time I was halfway down the sidewalk.

"Just wanted to say hello to your mother, John. Give her my congratulations."

He passed me as he walked up to the front door and knocked. I didn't go along, but I did watch. I was half afraid Mom would open the door and pass out; I didn't know when she'd last seen the guy. She did rock back on her heels a little, but then she steadied.

Dad was being a jolly good fellow; I could hear him blowing on about how wonderful it was she'd found someone and how he hoped she'd be happy, yadda, yadda, yadda. His best wishes... If Mom said anything, I couldn't hear it. In another minute Dad sailed back down the sidewalk with a determined look on his face, smacking his hands together. He'd gotten that job done.

We were always pretty quiet in the car. Dad would turn on NPR and listen to the news. Sometimes he'd comment on some natural disaster or political upheaval, and I'd feel obliged to murmur a noncommittal response. I don't know why I can't stand talking to him; I guess because I know he'd like me to. He'd probably like me to read all those dumb books his company publishes so we could have stimulating, literary conversations.

Since we're driving against the traffic that time of day, and since Dad drives like a bat out of hell anyway, we usually make it back to Marlborough Street in record time. But today he'd come up with this cuckoo idea of stopping for takeout before going back to his place. We'd have to eat in private. I couldn't remember the last time we'd done that. No restaurant noise to cover our silence, no menus to pretend to be interested in, no customers to pretend to watch. What would we *do*?

I was so distraught I gave in to the Chinese food idea. It's my father's favorite cuisine, so I naturally opt for almost anything else even though I like Chinese just fine. He called the order in on his car phone—(I'm glad practically everybody has them now so he can't feel so superior using the conspicuous thing)—so we could just zip by and pick it up on our way in.

"Let's eat at the table, like civilized folks, shall we?" he asked as he unlocked the door to his place. As though I had a choice. The big, polished table in the dining room was all ready for us—a table I'd never seen him use before except as an auxiliary desk when the one in his office was overflowing. But now there were two place settings all ready for us, napkins folded, wineglasses in back of the plates, and two brand new, never-burned candles in glass holders, waiting to be lit.

Was he getting ready to tell me some really bad news? Was he sick? Broke? Getting married too? No, not that. He used to tell Mom (in this annoyingly calm voice) that he never should have gotten married in the first place. He wasn't the kind of man who could be happy with an enclosed life. That's the way he put it: *an enclosed life*. Like he was so free now, Mr. Armani Suit, Mr. Car Phone, Mr. Take-Out Food.

He dumped the Moo Shu Pork, the Emerald Chicken, and the rice into bowls, put the scallion pancakes and steamed dumplings on a plate, and brought them to the table, as if he'd actually prepared dinner instead of just paying for it. He lit the candles, as if we were *celebrating* something. I'd be damned if I'd ask him what the hell was going on.

"This is nice for a change, isn't it?" He snapped the napkin and put it in his lap.

"What the hell is going on?" I couldn't help it; I was too nervous to eat.

He smiled but continued to spoon rice onto his plate. "You're perceptive, aren't you?" Perceptive? I'd have to be comatose not to smell a rat here. He sighed, but it wasn't an unhappy sigh. "The fact is, I sometimes feel like I don't know you anymore, John. We spend time together, but we don't talk much."

"Whose fault is that?" I mumbled. Now that I knew he just wanted to bullshit me, I could eat. The Moo Shu looked good, even with bullshit sauce ladled over it.

"I don't think we need to assign blame. The fact is, you're practically an adult now, and I'd like to think we can have a mature relationship. I thought about your outburst the other week, and I realized that I haven't been giving you enough credit, have I? You're a man now, and we should be able to speak to each other directly."

Oh, wow, I was so flattered. And wasn't it wise of him to plan a private chat this time, so his manly son couldn't embarrass him in public a second time? "So, what are you planning to say to me now that I'm a man that you couldn't say to me when I was a kid?"

He squeezed a dumpling between his designer chopsticks, took a big bite, and chewed carefully while he thought that one over. "What I'd like to talk to you about, John, is divorcing your mother. I hope you're old enough now to understand that I had no choice."

Whoa. I definitely was not old enough, and might not *ever* be old enough to hear why my father had no choice except to run off with one of his anorexic girlfriends and leave my mother sitting in the dark.

"And I'm not blaming your mother. I'm really not. But I had to get out of there, John. It was home to her, but it was killing me. That small-minded community, everyone so concerned about trimming their shrubs, and growing their roses, and, and..."

"Raising their kids?" I suggested.

He smiled at me, like he was proud I'd managed to zing him. "Well, that too, I suppose. I never was much of a soccer dad. Do you remember the first year you played baseball, Farm Team or something? You were about eight, I think, and the coach asked me if I'd help him, be an assistant. I had to laugh at the poor guy. He'd gotten himself roped into it, and now he was trying to get another sucker involved. No, sir." He shook his head at the guy's naïveté.

My appetite had suddenly disappeared. I poked at a dumpling with my chopsticks, ripping it to pieces, remembering how much I hated picking up that heavy bat and taking my turn at the plate, the opposing team screaming, "Easy out! Easy out!"

"Eight was too old to start baseball. All the other kids had played for years. I was never any good compared to them."

Dad swatted that complaint out of the air. "Oh, well, all that sports stuff is a waste of time anyway. You were too smart for baseball. You didn't need it."

"You mean *you* didn't need it."

"If you'd really wanted to play, your mother could have driven you."

"How was I supposed to know what I really wanted? I was eight. Besides, she did drive me to swimming lessons and karate lessons and day camp. She was busy too, you know. She worked. She had a life. You just didn't want anything to do with either of us. You were an urban hotshot, and we were too small town for you." I tossed the chopsticks aside.

"John, can you honestly tell me you enjoy living in Darlington? For children I suppose it's fine, but for someone your age, it must be deadly boring."

Of course it was boring, but I damn well wasn't going to admit it to him. "I guess it's boring for people who have no inner resources. It seems fine to me." I scooped up a big batch of Emerald Chicken, hoping that if I got my inner resources filled up a little more, they'd stop churning.

He gave me an exasperated look over the top of his glasses and maneuvered the last of the Moo Shu onto a pancake. "I can see this subject is still difficult for you. I'm sorry I brought it up. Let's forget it. I bought coffee ripple ice cream for dessert."

"Oh, well, that will make everything okay then. Yum yum. Real men eat ice cream."

That really cheesed him off. I was acting *so* immaturely. "John, I can do without the sarcasm."

"I know you can. You can do without me, too." I got up and smacked the chair into the table. "By the way, I

don't care what your excuse is. I'll never be old enough to
forget what it felt like when you walked out and left us."

Marisol was hunched so closely over the pages there was
barely room for her coffee cup to slip between the table and
her lips. I watched her narrow her eyes and sip. She was on
her third reading and had already shushed me once when I
tried to interrupt to ask what she thought. If I'd known she
was going to take it so seriously, I might not have even
brought the thing.

Finally she looked up, her finger stabbing at the page
before her. "There's the moment of truth," she said. "That's
what makes it worth reading."

"Yeah?" I leaned over the table to see what she was
pointing to.

"'All I know is I don't want anything else to change
right now.' That's the line that lets me know this cocky guy
is real, that he's not just a slick jerk who doesn't care about
anything."

I sat back in my chair. "You think I sound cocky and
jerky?"

"It's your style: cool, unmoved, seeing it all from a distance. Don't tell me that surprises you. This last
paragraph? You throw a tantrum, then reflect calmly on
how upset they'll be as you pick up an ice cream bar on
your way upstairs. Come on. You're not going for vulnera-
bility here."

"Well, why should I?"

"You shouldn't necessarily. But that style doesn't let your reader see much of the person behind the writing. Which is probably your intent. You're such a hidden person anyway."

"What?"

"Please, you aren't going to argue about *that*? You won't even decide if you're gay or not. You don't want any *information* attached to you; you don't want to give away any clues."

I felt like she'd pinned my wings to a board, and now she was zooming in with the microscope.

"When I read something, I like to feel I've gotten to know the writer a little bit," she continued. "For me, page after page of this kind of sarcasm gets annoying." She put her hand up. "Don't get me wrong. You write very well. *Very* well. It's funny and it's strong, and actually, I'm pretty impressed. If I wasn't, I'd just shut up about it."

"So you *liked* it? I'm having a hard time figuring this out."

"Yeah, I liked it, but the part that makes the rest of it work, for me, anyway, is the line about not wanting anything else to change. It just rings true. And because the rest of the piece is so guarded, it feels like it just slipped out, which makes it seem even more true. Do you see what I mean?"

I pulled the pages back to my side of the table. "I guess so." I couldn't even remember writing that line. Maybe it stuck out because it didn't really belong.

"You know what I'd really like to read is a rewrite of

your "Escape" piece that you read to me over the phone. That one I could start to *feel*."

"Yeah? I thought that was a mess, actually. I ditched it." I was lying to her again, without even giving it a second thought. The piece was right there, right in my backpack, but this crap about writing down my feelings was a crock. Like girls keeping a diary or something. That wasn't what a zine was about. Not mine.

Marisol waved to the waitress to bring more coffee. "Well, anyway, don't get all mad about it. I like your writing. Whoever you are." She almost smiled.

"So did you bring something for me to rip to shreds?"

"I tried."

"What? You didn't bring anything? Unfair!" Actually it was probably a good thing. Ever since my bout with Dad last night, I'd been kind of spoiling for another fight, as if liberating that little spurt of anger made all the rest of it frantic to escape too. Wouldn't be a good idea to unleash it on Marisol's writing.

"The thing is, I really want to write about a particular subject, something I can't seem to get a handle on. I spent most of the week trying to get started on it and then I threw it all away. It was too...personal."

"*Too* personal. I thought that was the whole point? You just told me..."

"I mean the details were too personal. There was a lot of pain just lying there on the page. That doesn't work either. I guess I don't have enough distance on it yet to understand it. Maybe I never will."

"Was it about...a girl?" I wasn't one hundred percent sure I wanted to hear some lesbian love story, but I did kind of want Marisol to tell me things about herself. I guess I wanted more clues to who she was too. Besides, I was tired of thinking about my own stupid problems.

She scanned the bookshelves. "Well, I'll give you the short version. The details are boring anyway. It was about six months ago. I'd only been out for a few months, but I met this group of girls who said they were lesbians. One of them goes to my school, and the rest go to other schools around here. Anyway, there was this one girl, Kelly. She was funny and smart. Right away I fell for her. It was the first time I really felt like that, you know? No, I guess you don't. Anyway, she flirted with me and we, you know, kissed and stuff. I was so happy. I thought I'd found the perfect person for me. She was so cool—she didn't let me get away with any of my G and T bullshit. My show-off stuff. She was just...great." Marisol stopped her story and started playing with the coffee cup.

"So, I guess she dumped you?" I know it was mean to cut to the chase like that, but I was kind of pissed off that she just assumed I couldn't possibly understand what it felt like to be crazy about somebody like that. I mean, it hasn't happened to me, but I read; I have an imagination. I think about it once in a while.

"Umm. But that wasn't even the worst. I mean, it was, but, the way it happened. We were sitting in Harvard Square one evening, listening to this Peruvian street band. It was kind of cold, and we were cuddled together, and I

was feeling so in love. Out in public and everything. I'd never felt like that before. Gio, you can't imagine how it feels when you've wanted someone as badly as I did, and thought you'd never find anybody, and then there she is— next to you—touching you!"

There was a raspy quality to her voice that was making my own throat close up. When Marisol looked at me I felt like she could see how I was put together, like I was one of those Invisible Man toys kids assemble so they can see how all their insides work. I wished her story was over already. I didn't want to hear anymore. All of a sudden I was scared, scared of the feelings she'd had, and I'd never had, and scared of what would happen next.

"We were sitting there together," she continued, "and I turned to her, to kiss her, and she looked down at me and said, 'You know, Marisol, I'm not really sure I'm a lesbian after all.' It turned out she'd been seeing this guy too, and she decided she really preferred the straight and narrow. Like homosexuality was just this *outfit* she was trying on, and it didn't quite fit. I never saw her again after that night."

I could imagine it. That feeling in your gut like every-thing's been pulled out and tied in knots, then stuffed back in any old way. That's how I'd felt when Dad left, when Mom disappeared into the dark.

Neither of us said anything for a minute, until finally I got my vocal chords to work. "That's awful."

"Yeah."

"You'll find another girlfriend, though."

She shrugged. "Maybe. I don't hang with the so-called lesbian group anymore. Mostly I just hang with Birdie. Or you now." She drained her cup. "I'd have to find somebody who's not a goddamn liar."

I trust the red sun setting,
the leafless November trees.
On monday morning I look forward
Fearlessly to Friday's eve.

But humans are not as reliable
as nature, as trees.
I wonder if you'll come back;
I trust only that you'll leave.

I hadn't written a poem for ages, but this one came spilling out while I sat on a bench in Copley Square after Marisol got on the subway home. At first I thought it was about Kelly leaving Marisol, but the more I worked on it, I realized it was really my own poem. Maybe about Dad leaving. Except I also kept seeing her, Marisol, heading down the stairs to the station, black bag riding low on her back, boot heels clicking away from me.

"I promised Birdie I'd hang with him next Saturday," she'd said. "He's jealous as hell. Two weeks, okay? Call me if you want to read me something."

Two weeks was forever. Maybe I would call, but I wouldn't read her the poem. She didn't lie. I didn't trust her.

Chapter Seven

The nuns were climbing every mountain and fording every stream while a small team of mothers made final adjustments to the hems of their habits, and the Von Trapp family escaped over the mountains and down the aisle of the Darlington High Little Theater.

For some reason that song about following rainbows and finding your dreams made the hair stand up on the back of my neck. I reminded myself Maria was only Violet Neville looking brave in a dumb hairdo, the captain was Vincent Brazwell carrying a small freshman on his back, and the Nazis were mostly kids who couldn't act very well. Brian was already poking me in the ribs.

"Aren't they great? The show's going to be cool, isn't it? You have to admit it, John."

"Which one is she again?" I said. I hate when people tell me I have to admit something to them.

"Top row on the left. I think they're done rehearsing anyway. You can meet her. Finally."

For some reason I was dreading meeting Brian's beloved freshman, Emily Prine. I'd been making excuses to him for weeks, but this was the final week of rehearsals before the show, and I couldn't keep it up without jeopardizing the only male friendship I had.

Brian was waving like crazy, and finally this tall, smiley girl with a shawl of curly red hair all down her back came running toward us, a wimple in her hand. A mother chased her down the aisle.

"Emily, give me your costume. We don't want it to get soiled before Friday night."

So Emily stood there disrobing while Brian introduced us. She had on a very short skirt (for a nun) and green tights over her thin legs, which gave her a Peter Pan-ish look.

"I'm *so* glad to finally meet you," Emily said. "Bri talks about you all the time."

"No, I don't!" Brian said.

Emily blushed. "I don't mean *all* the time, or anything. So, are you coming to the play this weekend? I hope!" I could tell she was basically kind of shy, but so excited about the play, and about having a boyfriend and everything, that she was pushing herself forward more than she ordinarily would have. Brian grabbed hold of her hand like it was going somewhere without him, the kind of proprietary move that always aggravates me. You are *mine*!

"Yeah, I guess so," I said. As long as I couldn't see Marisol this Saturday, what was the point of going into Boston at all? To be with dear old Dad? I was glad to have an excuse to stay in Darlington this weekend.

"Friday night or Saturday?" Brian asked.

"I don't know. Does it matter?"

"After Saturday's show there's a cast party. But if you go on Friday, we could hang around afterward or something."

There was a thrilling thought. They'd be giddy over the success of the play, and I'd have to listen to them recap all the little backstage traumas. "Did you notice when the lights came on too soon? Doodah couldn't find her so-and-so and she had to go *on*..." Besides, they were a couple now. Three's a crowd.

"I'm not sure yet. I'll have to let you know." Surely I could come up with some...lie. Man, I'd been lying more since I promised Marisol I wouldn't than I ever did before.

"You need a ride home, buddy? I've got wheels," Brian bragged. Wheels. He couldn't just say "the car." Of course

not. Brian was walking the borderline of cool now; he was approaching the wall of coolness with a blow torch.

"Sure. You can drop me off. Where do you live, Emily?" I asked.

"Um, just about a block from here. But Bri drives me anyway." She glanced at him sideways.

"Of course I do. And we take the long way." He tucked her hand in his jacket pocket, so he could find it again when he needed it. I only lived half a mile from the school but I wasn't at all sure I could stand to be in the car with the two of them for that long.

After I strapped myself in the back seat, I worked on becoming invisible, but Emily turned around politely. "So, John, who are you asking to the prom?"

God. I knew Brian had gotten an affirmative answer to the Big Question, but I thought I'd made my own feelings on the subject clear to him. "I'm not going. I'm not much for school activities."

"But Brian said we were doubling with you! We don't know who else to double with!"

"I never said..."

Brian looked at me in the rearview. "John, we talked about this. Remember? The thing is, none of Emily's close friends are going. I mean, they're freshmen; they don't have upperclass boyfriends." Emily wriggled happily in her seat; *she* had one. "And you're my best friend," Brian continued. "Who else would we go with?"

Best? *Only* would be closer to the truth. "You need a chaperone? Why can't you just go by your..."

"Oh, that's no fun!" Emily shouted. "I mean, it's a party. You want to be with friends!"

Jeez, Emily, calm down. "There's nobody for me to ask. I don't date anybody."

"Maybe Emily could fix you up with one of her friends. This weekend. Then if you liked her..."

"Yeah!" Emily was dancing all over the front seat, her hair smacking Brian in the face. "What a great idea! My friend Jessica! You'd love her! Don't you think, Bri? She's really cute and—"

"Wait! Hold on! I don't do fix-ups..."

"Yeah! Jessica!" Brian chimed in. Things were getting way out of control.

"No! No, really. I mean, maybe there is somebody I could ask. But no set-ups. Okay?"

Emily was disappointed; Brian curious. "Who would you ask? That Sarah person in pre-calc? I swear she's got the hots..."

How did this happen? I had no intention of going to the Junior Prom. "I don't know, Bri. Just let me think about it, would ya?" Thank God, we were at my house. My haven. My hiding place. I jumped out before Brian actually stopped the car.

"Great meeting you, Emily. Can't wait for the show." He smiled, happy to believe me. She was having a terrific freshman year.

"Call me, John," Brian insisted. "Let me know about the weekend and, you know, everything."

"Yeah, soon as I think it over." I ran inside and

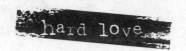

slammed the door on the two strangers who'd driven me home. I was so glad to escape from Beaver Cleaver and his girlfriend, it took me a minute to realize that my normally quiet home was booming with rock music. What the hell was this? ABBA? Blasting from the den?

Never has my mind been more blown than by the sight that greeted me when I walked into the den. There was my mother, my sober, somber mother, dressed in a T-shirt and a pair of those tight, shiny knee pants, pedaling like a maniac on the old stationery bike that had been sitting in the corner since Dad left. (I'd come to think of it as the correct place to hang a shirt I hoped she'd get around to ironing.) And she was singing, "Mamma Mia" at the top of her lungs.

She was too out of breath to hit the high notes, but she did seem to be enjoying herself. The music was so loud she hadn't heard me come in, so I thought I'd better sneak back out—she'd be embarrassed to know I witnessed this exertion, and I'd be embarrassed that she was embarrassed. But just then she turned around and saw me. I guess she always knows when another warm body is nearby; her security system is on alert lest I come too close.

The bike slowed down. "Oh, Johnny! Whew! I didn't hear you come in."

She didn't seem all that embarrassed. "I know. How come...?"

She climbed stiffly off the bike and lowered the volume on the stereo, then bent over at the waist to stretch out.

"Wow, I'm not used to this. I've been thinking lately I ought to put this bike to good use. It just sits here, and so do I, getting wider and wider."

I shrugged. "You look the same to me." Not that I paid much attention.

"I'm your mother; you wouldn't notice. But with the wedding coming up and everything...well, people look at you. You should make some effort."

Jeez, this wedding thing was a big deal to her. I guess I shouldn't have been surprised, but I was. She was trying to get in shape to be married, like it was the *big game* or something.

She was out of breath, but there was a little smile on her face as she rocked her hips back and forth to that song about the dancing queen. I looked past her, out the window, though I couldn't have told you what the hell was out there. It was too creepy to watch my mother acting like Jane Fonda in her sweaty little outfit.

"Your dad and I used to love this song. Doesn't that seem funny now? He's so sophisticated."

You could have knocked me over. Mom *never* talks about Dad, and certainly not like that, happy and remembering something nice about him. I had to get out of there—it was too confusing—so I headed for the kitchen. "I guess so," I called back. "By the way, I'm not going to Dad's this weekend."

I hadn't reached the fridge before she was on my tail, a little close for comfort, I would have thought.

"You aren't? How come? You go every weekend."

"I know, but Brian's play is this weekend. I told him I'd go."

"Both nights?"

"Well, no, but it seems silly to go into town for just one night. I mean, do I *have* to go every weekend? Believe me, Dad won't care." Whoops. That was a clue I didn't exactly want to give her, that Dad and I weren't on the best of terms.

But she didn't pick up on it; there was something else bothering her. "Well, no, you don't *have* to go. I just *assumed* you'd be gone, but..." She bit her lip.

I still didn't get it. "You don't want me around?" I said, laughing. "You planning something illicit?"

The look on her face: like I'd caught her with a needle in her arm or something. Then I got it. Of course. Al must come over on weekends. They sleep together here so his old mother doesn't get upset over there at the Haunted House. They can be alone here, but not if I stick around.

When she saw I was figuring it out, she rallied. "Of course there's no problem with you staying here for the weekend. It's your *home*, John."

"Actually, it's your home. Look, I don't care if Al stays here. You're going to be married to the guy pretty soon anyway. What difference does it make?" I thought I was being damn *mature* about the whole thing, especially since running into Al in the hallway in nothing but his Calvins was the grotesque image I was having to dislodge from my brain.

Mom turned around and got busy taking canisters out of the cabinet. "Hand me the margarine, would you, John?

I'll make some corn bread for supper. Wouldn't that be good? I haven't made corn bread for ages. I'll thaw out that chili I put in the freezer..."

Her sex life was obviously not going to be on the table for discussion. She'd slammed the window back down on communication. I should have appreciated the few minutes she let me peek in. She rattled on about food, grabbed the margarine tub with two finger pads so as to have no contact with her son's beefy hand.

I just stood there for a minute, hoping the heat of my sudden rage would scorch her too. What if I put these repugnant hands on her shoulders, or my arm around her waist, as old Al was certainly allowed to do? Probably every weekend for months now. Brian could kid around with his mother like that. She enjoyed it. But I couldn't because... because I was *his* son, contaminated.

"Why don't you go get your homework done before dinner?" she suggested. *Get out of here* was what she meant. I was happy to oblige. The sandpaper sound of her thighs brushing together in those oil slick shorts was making me sick.

As I picked up my pack where I'd dropped it in the den doorway, I heard ABBA belting out some song about how you couldn't escape even if you wanted to. Hah! That's what *they* think.

* * *

NO REGR

It occurs to me that in my first three issues I didn't explain the name of my zine. A couple of people have written to say that it's impossible to have "no regrets," so it's kind of a silly name. They tell me everybody has regrets unless they're some kind of Goody Two-Shoes. Unless their lives have been boringly trouble free. Unless they're just plain stupid.

First of all, I'm not stupid. I don't intend to publish my report cards here or some accolade from a teacher, so you'll just have to take my word for it. Whether I'm a Goody Two-Shoes or not, I can't say. For one thing, I don't really know what that is—somebody who's constantly happy or tirelessly helpful to everybody? If so, that's not me. I get tired and depressed just like everybody else. But if it means somebody who'd rather focus on the good stuff than wail about the bad, then I'll have to accept the silly name.

ADOPT MELLOW!

a b

As for having a trouble-free life, I haven't. I hate even telling people this because they're always so horrified by it, and don't know what to say to me, but in a zine I guess it's okay because you don't have to say anything back to me unless you want to. My mother died when I was ten years old. That was the biggest, worst thing. There was other stuff too—my dad kind of freaked out on booze for a while, and my older sister got crazy and wild. But those things straightened out, and we're all okay now. The only thing that can never change is death—that you just have to live with.

If you still have both your parents, you can't imagine how much it hurts when one of them dies, or how frightened you feel. I was so young I didn't really understand death (I guess I still don't), and I kept thinking my mother would come back somehow, even though I knew she couldn't. Maybe death is too big a thing for anybody to really get a

Protesting students for hanging of Suha

JAKARTA, Indonesia — About 3,000 stude
manded that ex-President Suharto be h
and his wealth seized after soldiers stop
them from marching on his house in the

handle on, but when you're ten and the person who dies is your mother who you love so much, it's like being in the middle of a tornado that just won't stop ripping you apart. Except that finally it does. Finally the wind dies down and you're still standing.

So you're probably saying, doesn't she regret that her mother died? Wouldn't she like to have her back? Of course I would, but my regrets won't accomplish that, will they? I don't regret my time in the tornado either, because it made me who I am today: someone who knows she can weather anything. So when I say "no regrets" I mean there's no reason to look back, wishing you could change things. I do look back with sadness sometimes, but just as often I remember the happy times I had with my mother. And I always look to the future with hope. If you have no regrets, you stop wishing you could rearrange your past, and you start looking forward to whatever is up ahead.

—Diana Tree

Okay. seen it of us loved i do. Bu need to fairy t Here ar

That was the first page of the new issue of *No Regrets* I'd picked up over the weekend. Not the kind of run-together, first-thing-that-comes-to-my-mind stuff that she usually wrote, but, even more than her other writing, it gave me the feeling I really *knew* this Diana person. Like she was telling me all this stuff in a conversation with me alone, not in a zine read by a hundred other people. Not that I really believed what she was saying. But I believed *she* believed what she was saying.

Without giving it much thought, I sat down at the computer and went into my word-processing program. I wrote:

Dear Diana,

Why is it that people don't know what to say when something bad has happened to someone they know? Maybe because they think there are some magic words that will make everything all right again, only they don't know what the words are. They ought to understand that there isn't anything right to say. Mostly they need to just sit there and listen.

When my father walked out on my mother, her best friend didn't want to talk about it. I remember she kept saying (I was always in the next room, listening to everything the adults said, trying to figure it all out), "Let's not dwell on it, Anne. Don't get down in the dumps." Those weren't the magic words. My mother started hanging around with another woman she knew who'd listen to her sad story over and over, about how she never saw it coming, how she didn't know if she'd survive. (I guess she was in a kind of tornado too.)

She did survive, but I think she'd say she has some regrets, even now, when she's planning to get married again. I have some regrets too. Can't help it. I wish she'd married someone else to begin with. Of course, I'd be a different person, but how bad could that be? Without the part of me contributed by my father, maybe I'd be less of a jerk. I'm pretty sure being a jerk is genetic, so it's probably lucky I don't have any siblings.

I don't think you're stupid or a Goody Two-Shoes. I do think it's kind of amazing that you're so optimistic about life, considering what you've gone through. From the outside my life probably looks like it's been a lot easier than yours, but it still seems to me that it basically sucks. Why do you think you didn't let the whole thing get you down? I'd really like to know. I guess you can tell: I'm looking for magic words too.

I like *No Regrets* a lot. Another good zine is *Escape Velocity*—have you ever seen it? My friend Marisol Guzman writes it. I'm enclosing a copy of my zine, *Bananafish*, in case you're interested.

I spent a long time trying to decide how to sign the thing (or whether to mail it at all), and then finally I just signed it: John Galardi, a.k.a. Giovanni. I had to stop all this lying about dumb stuff like my name. I mean, there might be a good reason to lie about something important from time to time, but not about stuff like that. And besides, I already told her who I was in the letter. Having an ethnic name wasn't going to change whatever opinion she already had. Besides, I'd never meet her anyway.

Chapter Eight

I went to hear the nuns sing both nights. What else was there to do? Since my room in Darlington wasn't as well equipped as the one on Marlborough Street, I had to leave it periodically, which meant the possibility of running into Al, which was fairly uncomfortable even if he wasn't in his underwear. Rather than feel like a prisoner in my own home, I escaped.

The play was corny as hell, of course, but I kind of enjoyed it anyway. What a riot to see Brian up there, bowing and yes-sirring so seriously. Vincent Brazwell's voice was pretty grating, but Violet was passable, and those damn nuns were actually good. That last song, every time I heard it, I had to look away and think about something else. For some reason, even though I *knew* these were a bunch of high school kids whose idea of courage was taking advanced placement physics, I couldn't stop thinking about the real people who had to leave everything behind them and hike out of their country at night with only the

few things they could carry. I don't know what's the matter with me lately. It's like that sad/hopeful stuff gets to me a little bit.

So there I was Friday night, feeling kindly toward the butler and the nun as we sat in a booth at the coffee shop at midnight. Of course, Emily started talking about the prom again and how she could help me get a date. I guess what happened was I felt like such a loser sitting there across from Romeo and Juliet. If you want the truth, I suppose I always felt a little bit superior to old Brian. Like I could have gotten dates if I'd wanted to, but he, who was dying to go out with a girl, couldn't even get a female to speak to him. Well, Emily was speaking to him, and apparently a whole lot more.

So one minute I'm sitting there trying to figure out how to get out of this prom thing altogether, and the next I hear a fully developed story coming out of my mouth I didn't even know I was cooking up. Apparently I've now become a completely incorrigible liar.

"Actually, I do have a girlfriend," I said. "In Boston. I've been seeing her on weekends when I stay at Dad's. That's why I haven't wanted you to come in with me lately, Bri." Didn't that sound absolutely plausible?

"You do?" Brian's eyes were round as Ping-Pong balls. "Why didn't you tell me?"

Easy. "Well, I didn't want to make you feel bad. I mean, this started before you met Emily, so..." What a friend.

"I've been going with Emily for weeks already. You

could have told me. How'd you meet her?" Brian looked kind of hurt, but Emily was only curious.

"What's her name? What's she like? Is she coming to the prom?"

All of sudden I panicked. Where was this lie headed? "Her name is...Marisol. I met her at Tower Records; she's a zine writer, like me." No lies there.

"A what writer?" Emily wrinkled up her face.

"Zines. They're like homemade magazines," Brian explained. "Only you just put your own writing in it." I had given Brian a copy of my first issue, so now he was a font of knowledge, even though he probably hadn't even read the thing.

"Wow. You both do that? How cool!" Emily was impressed by *anything*. She dumped a fourth packet of sugar into her cappuccino, which made me a little more sympathetic toward her than I had been.

"Anyway, that's how I met her, and now we go out almost every weekend. Not this weekend, since I stayed here for the play."

"I bet she's mad," Emily said.

I shrugged. "We don't *own* each other." Apparently Emily couldn't see my nose expanding like zucchini in August, but I suspected Marisol would take it in at a glance.

"So, you asked her to the prom, then?" Brian looked suspicious.

Some fast talking would be needed now. "Well, that's the thing. I mean, Marisol is very cool, you know? She's a city person. We like to just hang out in Boston, take in the

scene. She's not really the prom type, if you know what I mean."

"Thanks a lot, John!" Emily let her mouth hang open in mock shock. "I guess we're just not cool enough for Marisol. We're *prom types*."

"That's not what I meant..."

"I am so sick of this Mr. Cool attitude, you know that?" Brian said, shoving his empty cup across the table. "For years I've had to listen to you dis everything and everybody because you think you're better than they are. Well, you're no better than the rest of us slobs, John. You're not!"

Just then a bunch of other actors from the play came in (nuns and Nazis, not stars) and rushed over to exchange hugs and kisses with Brian and Emily, like we were all on Broadway or something. Not one of them had managed to get all the makeup off their face, but I figured they probably liked it that way, so people could see what professional stage-meisters they were. It was weird to see Brian so comfortable around people I didn't even know. He wasn't alone anymore; he had friends, interests, Emily.

When the actors went to their own booth, I apologized. "I just meant I feel funny asking her to the prom. I don't know. Maybe she'll go, but if she doesn't want to, I don't want to go with anybody else." That sounded good.

"But you'll ask her?" Brian prodded. "It's not going to kill you to ask her."

"Okay, okay, I'll ask her," I said, promising myself this was my last major lie. When I told them later that she didn't want to go, it would be gospel truth.

"What kind of name is Marisol?" Emily asked, happy again.

"Spanish, I guess. She's originally from Puerto Rico."

"Oh, my God, she sounds so awesome! I can't wait to meet her!"

An event, I decided, which must never take place.

Of course, there was no reason to even mention this silly prom business to Marisol herself. But then Saturday turned out to be such a terrific day. Marisol came flying down the block toward me as I walked up Newbury Street. I'd kind of forgotten in two weeks how amazing she looked. And here she came, running to see *me*.

"Guess what? Are you busy tonight? Do you want to go to a concert with me?" She waved tickets in my face. "I can't believe I got two tickets. My mother got them from some client of hers who's in the record biz. She's trying to get on my good side. This might just do it, too. Can you believe it?"

I was trying to see what band was printed on the tickets, but she kept waving her arm around and I couldn't see. "Hold still!" I said, grabbing her wrist. "What concert?"

"Ani. Ani DiFranco. At the Orpheum. You know her, don't you?"

I read the name on the ticket. "Doesn't ring a bell. Who is she?"

Marisol let her head fall back and looked for heavenly inspiration to describe her idol. "Omigod, she's so incredible.

Her voice is like a razor. She's a poet, really. She writes this beautiful stuff that just blows me away."

I guess I didn't seem overly excited.

"You don't wanna go? I'm offering you a free ticket to the best concert you'll see this year, and you don't wanna go? Fine!" She grabbed the tickets out of my hand. "I'll call Birdie. I thought I was doing you a favor, but..."

"Hold on a minute. I didn't say I didn't want to go. I just never heard of her."

"She's an independent. They don't play her stuff on those trashy rock stations you probably listen to." She was glaring up at me from under her spiky bangs.

"Marisol, if you say she's good, I believe you. Besides, I'd want to go even if she was awful. The more time I spend with you, the less time I spend at Dad's place."

"Oh, thanks for the compliment. You like me more than your father, the lecher, but less than...what? Your grandmother, the jewel thief?" She was warming up again.

"No. You beat out Granny, too. Besides, she's not a jewel thief; she's an ax murderer."

Wow. A real smile. Held down at one corner, of course, and kind of squished up into her nose so that I wouldn't think she was really feeling kindly toward me, but still, a smile.

Suddenly her voltage meter shot up even higher. "Oh! I almost forgot my *other* good news: I got into Stanford!"

"You did? That's great. In California, right?" I said, feeling a lot less happy than I had a few seconds before.

"California!" she said dreamily. "Land of escape!"

"Have you ever *been* there? I mean, how do you know you'll like it?"

"Gio, I would like any place that's three thousand miles from here."

I tried not to take it personally. "Because of your parents, you mean? They won't be looking over your shoulder all the time."

"That, sure. But I'm tired of the East Coast too. I want a change. Change makes things happen, you know?" Her shoulders trembled with excitement as she looked into the future.

"I wouldn't know," I said crabbily. "I live in Darlington, remember? We're allergic to change."

"You'll get out too. You're too good a writer to get stuck in the suburbs. Think big, Gio! Imagine what comes next and make it happen!"

That picked me up again, Marisol saying I was a good writer. Listening to Marisol talk, you started to believe a terrific future was a real possibility and not just some childish fantasy.

After our usual coffee, we went to the Institute of Contemporary Art (Marisol's idea), where they had a group show of local artists. Going to a gallery is not something I usually do; as a matter of fact, I'd never gone to one before. Oh, yeah, Dad had dragged me to the Museum of Fine Arts a few times when I was a kid, but he gave up taking me places years ago. Walking around the ICA made me feel grown-up in a funny way. I mean, I didn't exactly know why people went to art museums—how are you supposed to look at

paintings and what do you say about them?—but being there with Marisol was so cool. She *belonged* in that kind of place.

"Look at these colors. Don't you love this—the way she drapes this form around that one? With that yellow? I always wanted to paint, didn't you?"

"No. I was never any good at art."

"I'm not either; I just want to do everything. Why can't we all do everything we want to? I'd be a writer and a singer and a painter and a politician and...maybe an Olympic track star."

"In one lifetime?"

"Why not? Sleep less."

By the middle of the afternoon we were back at Tower Records, looking at zines. Marisol went inside to the non-freebie racks, and I followed after a few minutes. She'd already found what she was looking for.

"You're in *Factsheet 5*!" She held the magazine out to me.

"A review?"

"A good one! Read it."

I was so excited I could hardly hold the floppy newsprint still, barely make my eyes focus on the small type. But there it was:

Bananafish #1

I was impressed with this funny, irreverent peek into Giovanni's psyche. The poetry got a little obscure sometimes, but the recipe for "Mother Soup" ("1/2 teaspoon Random Act of Kindness for every 2 cups of Self-Sacrifice. Serve in unused running shoes.") was hilarious. My favorite piece, "Interview with the Stepfather," was wise and witty and even a little poignant when Boy admits his real father's ineptitude. A slim first issue but look for more good stuff from this guy. Will trade. Price: $1 and 2 stamps. Giovanni, P.O. Box 98, Darlington, MA.

"Not bad, huh? Almost as good as *my* first review," Marisol said.

"What's he mean, 'poignant'?" I asked.

"He means it goes deep. It's touching. It's not an insult, Gio."

"I didn't mean for it to be *touching*."

Marisol rolled her eyes. "Oh, God, don't tell me you left your closet door open a crack and somebody looked in! What were you thinking?"

"Ha, ha."

"Gio, this is a great review. People will want to read *Bananafish* now. Are you complaining?"

"No! I'm just...surprised. It *is* good, isn't it?"

She shook her head and gave me an elbow in the ribs. "Buy it and then let's go have a celebratory dinner before the concert. Because we are such total winners, and because I'm starving to death." For a small person she sure liked to eat.

I called and left a message on Dad's machine that I'd be out late at a concert (as though he'd care), and we went in search of a Thai restaurant Marisol remembered. It was small and dark and partly underground.

A waiter seated us at a table in the corner, lit the candle, smiled kindly. I let Marisol order because I wasn't that familiar with Thai food.

"How come you know so much? I mean how to talk about art, and what to order in a Thai restaurant, and the difference between *caffè latte* and *café con leche*. Really. You're not even a year older than I am, and I don't know any of that stuff."

She shrugged. "I don't know. Maybe it's growing up in Cambridge. My mother's from one of those cosmopolitan-type families where everybody instinctively knows how to handle any situation with ease by the time they're three years old. You can't shock or surprise them. They *know* too much. I hope I'm not like that. I hope I can still be surprised."

"Like the way your mother handled it when you came out to her."

"Right. She read some books, made a few phone calls, and within twenty-four hours she knew more about homosexuality than I did. Wait, how did you know that?"

"Read it in *Escape Velocity*."

She laughed. "God, I put my whole life down in print, and then forget people actually *read* it. It's a little scary. I mean, you know things I wouldn't ordinarily tell somebody I didn't know very well."

I must have gotten a funny look on my face or something. I mean, it did hurt me a little bit because I was thinking we knew each other pretty well now.

"Don't pout," Marisol said. "You're the only straight guy I would *ever* invite to an Ani DiFranco concert. And here's another thing I wasn't going to tell you: The one and only other time I ate in this restaurant was with Kelly." She frowned into the candle flame. "So let's make it memorable. I want to wash that other evening out of my mind."

It was memorable, at least for me. We talked about all kinds of things. I told her about the argument I'd had with Dad two weeks ago, about Mom riding the exercise bike

and listening to ABBA, about the singing nuns and Brian's new confidence. She told me about how she used to go fishing with her father, and to the opera with her mother, and how she'd raised cockatoos on their sun porch for three years. And then, somehow, just as we were cleaning up the last of the *pad Thai*, we got onto the topic of our high schools, which made me think about the stupid prom, and then, before I knew it, the unthinkable question popped out of my mouth.

"Speaking of high school, you wouldn't be willing to go to the Junior Prom with me in two weeks, would you?"

Just the look on her face made little bubbles of sweat burst through my skin. Now I'd ruined everything.

"What?" she whispered, leaning across the table as though she couldn't possibly have heard me correctly.

"I don't want to go that much myself, but my friend, Brian..."

"Okay, I'm still capable of surprise! Gio, do I look like a person who goes to a *prom*?" She pulled at her hair spikes. "No offense to darling Darlington, but God, Gio. Why would *anybody* want to go to a dorky, suburban prom? I never thought *you* would."

I never thought I would either, but listening to Marisol put the place down like that, I had to defend it a little bit. "It's not the ninth circle of hell, Marisol. It's twenty-five minutes from Boston, not in some backwoods somewhere."

"So?"

"So, I just thought it might be fun to do something... normal. For a change. Just to see what it's like."

"And you think it's normal to date a lesbian?"

"It wouldn't be a *date*. A lot of people go with friends. You don't have to be engaged."

"A prom is...romantic. You have to dance. I'd have to wear a dress. A *fancy* dress. I'd have to do some kind of Barbie number, with hair and makeup. Lesbian Barbie—that would be cute. Gio, how can you ask me to do this?"

Why had it ever seemed like a plausible plan? "Okay. So it was a bad idea."

Marisol shivered her shoulders. "I mean, like *spaghetti* straps or something."

"Let's drop it. I had a moment of temporary insanity. You aren't going. I'm not going. We are both definitely not going."

"Gio, if you want to go, you should ask somebody who'd enjoy it. Some girls are *dying* to do this stuff. It's all they talk about."

"They aren't dying to do it with me."

She smacked her hand on the table. "Oh, please. You're such a monster? They should be happy somebody with a mind asks them out, instead of the usual brain-dead example of masculinity."

I shrugged. "There's nobody I really want to go with anyway. Most of the girls in my high school are such... girls."

"Gio, you are radically confused."

"I know."

She ordered us a sweet rice pudding dessert to cheer me up, which was nice of her. I guess she could tell I was

kind of hurt, but she didn't make too big a deal out of it. Later, as we walked to the Orpheum, it was just starting to rain a little. It was a warm night for April, and there were lots of people out on the street. It made me feel like things weren't so hopeless, like I wasn't the biggest fool on earth, like summer was coming and proms weren't important and Marisol was all the friend I needed. She started to sing some Ani DiFranco lines for me.

> "the more you talk
> the more I get
> the sense of something
> that hasn't happened yet..."

"That's from one of my favorite songs. Isn't it great? I get that feeling sometimes, like something is getting ready to change, something important is getting ready to happen. Do you ever get that feeling?"

"I do. Actually I have it now." I wasn't lying either.

"Really? There's another part in that song that reminds me of you," she said hesitantly.

> "i am so many white people
> i mean where do I start
> i got lots of personalities
> i just can't tell them apart."

"That's me? A WASP with multiple personalities?"

"Um hmm. And always asking, 'Where do I start?'"

"Well, where *do* I start?"

Marisol grabbed my arm almost roughly, then slid her black-gloved hand around my elbow. "You've started already, white boy. You just don't know it."

Chapter Nine

A cloud of smoke swirled through the crowd as we jostled our way outside, everybody lighting up as soon as they hit the lobby. All around us people were calling to each other, pushing past to reach old friends, or maybe they were people who barely knew each other, but now, meeting at an Ani concert, they recognized each other as soul mates.

It was a very good concert, and I had that after-a-good-concert feeling: the world can't be *such* a rotten place if I'm surrounded by this many people who appreciate the same artist I do. The music had been loud and exhilarating, and I was definitely an Ani fan now. I felt like I'd made some kind of electric connection with her, but then everybody else must have felt that way too. All around us people seemed really wired as they came down into the lobby.

It was raining a little more heavily than when we walked over, but it was still warm enough that you didn't mind too much. The scene outside the theater was very mellow, everybody circling around like they didn't want to leave yet, didn't want to admit it was over. Marisol came outside and immediately put her hands up in the air and belted out the first lines of an Ani song about walking in the rain.

Several people joined in or whooped or said, "You go, Girl." There were more women than men in the crowd, and probably more gay people than you'd find in a random sample too.

"Shit! Look what time it is!" Marisol said suddenly.

"Twelve thirty. What's the matter? You lose your glass slipper?"

"I missed the last Red Line train to Cambridge. Damn it! I promised my parents I'd make that train. They'll be really pissed off about getting out of bed to drive over here in what they refer to as 'the middle of the night.' Maybe I could walk home."

"To the other side of Harvard Square? By yourself? In the middle of the night?" She weighed ninety pounds; perverts would come out of the cracks in the sidewalk.

"You wanna walk with me?"

"No."

"My hero."

"It's too far." An idea surfaced in my brain that seemed to have been there all along. "Why don't you just stay at my dad's place overnight? He won't even know. He wouldn't care anyway."

Marisol bit the inside of her lip and thought it over. Apparently we were both mulling over the same question. "Where would I sleep?"

I was ready. "You can have my bed. I'll put a sleeping bag on the floor."

"I'll use the bag."

"I don't mind using the bag."

"I don't either."

I shrugged. "Whatever you want." I meant that sincerely. She could call the shots. Because as soon as the idea occurred to me, I began to anticipate it eagerly. Not because I thought anything sexual would happen (between a lesbian and a neuter?); I just didn't feel like saying good night to her yet. I wanted to be her closest friend, closer than Birdie, someone with whom she'd be comfortable sleeping in the same room.

Marisol stuck a strand of hair in the corner of her mouth and chewed another minute. "Okay. I'll take the bed. But just so you know ahead of time, there's no way I'm inviting you to share it. I don't care how uncomfortable the floor is. Are we clear on that?"

"Man! Give me some credit, will you? I *offered* to sleep on the floor. I *know* you're a lesbian, okay? You don't let me forget it for a minute."

"No? Sometimes I'm afraid I do."

We went back inside, and she called her parents from the lobby phone. I didn't want to eavesdrop, but it seemed to go pretty smoothly.

"So, they're all right with it?"

She grunted. "I think they're thrilled."

"That you missed the train?"

"That I'm staying with a *boy*." She shook her head.

"Sorry."

"As long as *you're* not thrilled."

That was a little too close for comfort, but I finessed it. "Hey," I said, "I'm totally bummed about the whole thing.

Filthy sleeping bag. Floor like fossilized stone. This suspicious crab-ass in my bed."

She belted me with one of those skinny, hard elbows, then broke into another Ani song as we headed back to Marlborough Street. We were pretty wet by the time we got there. Dad wasn't home, of course, so we took turns showering. I gave her a pair of Dad's pajamas to put on, but they were so big on her that the top alone was longer than most women's dresses. She had to roll the sleeves up about eleven times.

"Your dad actually wears silk pajamas?"

"I don't ask him, Marisol. I don't like to imagine what his bedtime behavior entails."

I'd put clean sheets on my bed while Marisol was in the shower, so she crawled in between Dad's Ralph Lauren plaids. Before she did though, I got a quick look at her legs. I couldn't help being curious; all she ever wears is pants. They were muscley, and covered with a thin layer of fine, black hair.

"So, does he have girlfriends over while you're here?" she asked, pulling the blanket up over her knees.

"It's happened. Usually he stays at their places, though."

"Wild!"

"It's not *wild*. He's just an old fart trying to act like he's twenty again. I think it's disgusting." I could just imagine him walking in on this scene: the girl tucked in the bed, and me on the floor in sweatpants and a T-shirt, cuddled up with my pillow. He'd laugh his ass off.

"You never talk to him about this stuff?"

"Are you kidding?"

"You know what you should do? You should write letters to him. I don't mean you should send them, just write
them. Put down everything you ever wanted to say to him,
good or bad."

"Why would I do that?"

She shrugged. "My therapist suggested it. Since I write
all the time anyway, she said I should try writing letters to
my mother. My birth mother."

"I didn't know you saw a therapist."

"My mom's a therapist, so, you know, she believes in
them. She got me started with Claire around the time I
came out, although what we usually end up talking about is
being adopted. Anyway, writing the letters has helped me
figure out who my mother is. Or, at least, who she isn't."

"Who isn't she?"

"She's not me. Which you might think is obvious, but
it isn't. When I talk to her like that, in a letter, she becomes
real, and I can get mad at her, and then, you know..." She
looked down at her tar-painted fingernails and lowered her
voice. "...forgive her. I write to her a lot. I wrote a letter this
morning in the Trident before you came."

"You did? Can I read it?"

She screwed up her face. "No! It's too personal!"

"So who do you show it to? Your therapist?"

She shook her head. "Not usually. Only if I want to.
She doesn't *grade* me or anything."

I glanced at her backpack, where it lay in the corner.

"Is it in there?" I said, grinning. I guess I just wanted to lighten the mood a little.

"Gio! Don't you dare!" She leaped up and crawled across the bed.

I thought she knew it was just a joke. I got to my knees and reached out toward the pack; I could have grabbed it if I'd wanted to. But Marisol wasn't laughing. She smacked my forehead with the back of her hand, which I wasn't expecting, and I sprawled backward on the sleeping bag. She jumped off the bed and grabbed her pack, hugging it to her chest like a wounded child.

"I can't believe you'd *do* that, Gio. I trusted you!" Her voice was shaking and cracking like I'd perpetrated a major betrayal.

"Do what? I was kidding, for God's sake. Shit, you really creamed my head." There were two little trails of blood where her black nails had grazed flesh. "I don't want to read your silly letter."

She stood in the corner glaring at me for another minute while I wiped my face with a tissue.

"I didn't think you would act like that, like one of those high school boys who tease all the time. I didn't expect it."

"Yeah, well, I'm glad to see we've built up such a trusting relationship." I hurled the red-spotted square in the direction of the trash can.

"Listen, I'm here, aren't I?" She stashed the pack at the side of the bed away from me, then crawled back under the covers. "Did I hurt you?"

"I'll live."

She sighed. "Let's just go to sleep. It's late."

"Fine." I got up and turned off the overhead light, then folded myself into the green nylon bag.

"Good night," Marisol said.

"'Night."

I heard her turn over on her side, away from me, and I did the same. The little slices on my forehead burned, but I knew it was from anger more than any real damage she'd done. I was wide awake and so mixed-up I suddenly wanted to scream.

"I hope you don't intend to finish me off in the middle of the night," I spit out. "You don't have a blade in that top secret backpack, do you?"

She didn't answer, didn't even rustle the covers. I turned onto my back and stared at the ceiling where a column of streetlamp light sliced an angle. No way was I going to be able to fall asleep while she lay three feet away thinking I was some high school chump. Maybe it was just too much to expect a straight guy and a lesbian to be best friends.

Ten minutes must have passed. I knew Marisol was still awake too; she was lying so motionlessly I wasn't sure she was even breathing. Finally I couldn't take it anymore.

"Look, I'm sorry," I said. "Don't be mad at me for such a dumb thing."

She snorted. "Why *should* I be mad at you, then?"

"You shouldn't. I'm harmless."

"I doubt that. But I guess I'll forgive you anyway."

"Thank you. Now you apologize."

She turned over to face me. "What for?"

"Drawing blood!"

"What a baby," she said, but her voice had relaxed; she wasn't angry anymore. "Fine. I'm sorry I mutilated your gorgeous face."

"You're forgiven. Now we can sleep."

"Thank you. Good night."

"Good night."

I guess I really was relieved, because I started to drift off as soon as we'd hammered out the peace accord. I was in that happy, half-dreaming place when Marisol's voice pulled me back to wakefulness.

"If you really want to hear it, I'll read it to you."

"What?"

"The letter. If you really want to hear it." She clicked on the little light next to the bed.

I had to shield my eyes for a minute. As a matter of fact, by that time I was too tired to give a damn about the letter, but not so stupid as to admit it. "Sure. I want to hear it."

She dug around in the pack and brought out a thick red notebook that had the legend "Letters to my Mother" inked on the cover. She opened it to the latest entry.

"I don't write these for anybody to read, so it's just what I'm thinking. It doesn't necessarily make sense, so don't expect..."

"I have no expectations. Just read it." I stacked two pillows against the wall so I could sit up and listen (and so there was less chance of my falling asleep on her).

But once she started to read, I was wide awake.

"'To my mother, whoever and wherever she is,'" she began, then stopped to explain, "I always start it out that way." I nodded and she continued.

Maybe you think it isn't fair that I write to you and complain about my life as an adoptee (which you probably think sounds just great and why am I complaining anyway) when I never write letters to my birth father, never blame him the way I blame you. Really I don't think that much about him. Maybe he didn't even know you were pregnant. I know society always lets the guy off the hook and blames the mother for any child-related problems, and that's wrong and I don't mean to do it. But I just don't have any picture of him in my mind. Whereas, you I see plainly, a young, brown woman handing her baby over to strangers.

Probably that's not fair either—how can I possibly know what the circumstances were when you were pregnant with an unwanted child? I suppose I should thank you for not having an abortion. Okay. I will. Thank you. But I don't thank you for this: that it's almost impossible for me to really trust anyone.

I know it goes back to being adopted; I know this. I'm a confident person, I have loving parents, I am, for God's sake, "gifted and talented." And some days I'm crazy about myself.

But somewhere down deep I think people don't really want to be with me. And if I let them see that I like them (as I did with Kelly), they'll run away (as she did, as you did). I'm afraid to have another girlfriend—I don't even look for one, because I wouldn't trust her anyway.

I spend my time with Birdie and Gio now, but sometimes I'm even afraid with them. Mom gave me two tickets to a concert for tonight, and I'll ask Gio to go with me. We have fun together, and sometimes I almost trust him. Since the tickets are free, he'll probably go, but maybe not. It means spending an entire day with me, which is probably a lot more than he bargained for. He likes to talk to me about writing, but he didn't sign up to be my best friend. Nobody ever does, which might be my own damn fault, but, Mother dear, today I feel like blaming you.

                    Your daughter,
                    Marisol Guzman

I can't explain all the thoughts and feelings that were buzzing through my body. It was almost too much information to take in all at once, but I wanted to take it in; I was thrilled that Marisol was giving it to me. I forced myself to stay there on the floor where I was, even though I wanted to touch her, to reassure her. But what would touching her mean? I imagined my hand on hers would jolt us like an

electrical shock, sending us running in opposite directions. For a minute we both sat in silence, although I was anything but quiet inside.

"Now you know why I didn't want you to read it," she said at last, not looking at me. "Okay. Time for bed." She reached over and clicked out the light, then slid back down under the covers.

I was glad the light was out. It helped me think what I wanted to say.

"Thanks for reading it to me. Really."

"Yeah, yeah."

"I have just one question. Where's the sign-up sheet?"

"What sign-up sheet?"

"Where I sign up to be your best friend."

She didn't say anything for a second, but I thought her breathing sounded a little ragged. "Go to sleep, goofball," she said finally.

"I'll see you in the morning," I promised.

"Not if I see you first," she said, pretending to be the grumpiest girl in the world.

He must have been standing right outside my door. "Wake up in there! Hot coffee and croissants from the bakery!"

What in the hell was going on? Usually I didn't even *see* my dad on Sundays until the middle of the afternoon when he was ready to drive me back to Darlington. I grabbed the clock off my night table: 10:08 A.M.

Then I heard Marisol groaning and twisting in the cov-

ers, and it came back to me suddenly why I was sleeping on the floor. Jesus! How was I going to get her out of there without running into Dad?

"Marisol!" I called up to the lump in the bed. "My Dad's up! He wants me to have breakfast with him!"

"Who's stopping you?" she mumbled.

Maybe if I went out and had a cup of coffee, he'd leave me alone, and Marisol could sneak out later. "I'll be back," I told her, pulling a flannel shirt on over the T-shirt I'd slept in. I eased out the door and closed it behind me.

Dad was in the kitchen arranging pastries on a big platter, enough for a half dozen people, it looked like. "You're up kind of early, aren't you?" I asked him.

"John!" he bellowed.

God. Why hadn't I thought about this problem?

"Where's your friend?" he asked.

"What friend?" He really caught me off guard.

The old turnip gave me this sly grin. "You thought I wouldn't notice those size two black jeans hanging over the shower rail?"

Damn it; why hadn't I thought of that? "Oh, yeah. Well, she's still asleep."

His eyes grazed my forehead, and he smiled. Before I could stop it, my hand flew guiltily up to check on the twin trails, skinny but swollen.

"What's her name?"

"Uh, Marisol. Look, Dad, this is going to sound crazy, but could you call me Gio while she's here? The thing is, she thinks..." This was too humiliating; he was chuckling already.

"Gio? Like in Giovanni?"

"It's not that important." Who cared? She was bound to find out anyway.

"No, no, Son. Whatever you say. I don't want to screw your thing up for you."

Screw my thing up? This was getting ridiculous. I hadn't seen the old bum so happy in years. I guess he was thinking, "like father, like son," or some such bull.

"Do I smell coffee?" Dad and I turned around so fast we bumped into each other. There was Marisol, puffy-eyed, wearing my father's pajama top, her hair relaxed around her face as if it hadn't woken up enough to get mad. Dad got this goofy grin on his face, and it occurred to me he was kind of excited to see a young woman inside his own slinky sleepwear.

"Good morning!" he said jovially. "Hot coffee for the little lady, coming up!"

Man. I waited for Marisol to start fuming over the "little lady" crack, but she just smiled uncertainly, her weight shifted onto one hip.

"Gio, have you got a bathrobe or something? It's a little chilly."

"Sure!" I raced back into my room and came out with the ratty, gray robe I'd had for years, from the time it was way too big for me until now, when it barely tied around my waist. It was plenty big for Marisol though, and I liked to see her snuggled into it.

"Sit down, kids." Dad put the mugs and the pastry plate on the island between the kitchen and the dining

room, pointed to the stools surrounding it. Marisol picked up her coffee and downed half a cup of scalding liquid before she sat.

Dad refilled her immediately. "So, Marisol, why haven't I met you before?" He was grinning at her in this smutty way. It seemed pretty lousy to me to have my father so deliriously pleased that I'd spend the night with a girl.

"This is the first time I've been here." She wasn't going to give anything away. She thought maybe I wanted him to think what he was obviously thinking.

"Well, you're welcome any time," he oozed.

"Thanks." She smiled politely, the perfect girlfriend.

"I didn't know *Gio* had been dating anyone."

"We've known each other a few months," Marisol told him, careful not to lie, only to tell the truth incompletely.

The whole stupid conversation was making me sick. I downed my coffee a.s.a.p. "Marisol, you need to be some-place this morning, don't you?"

She searched my face, trying to figure out the right answer. "Right. Thanks for reminding me. I'll finish my cof-fee while I get dressed." She scurried into the bathroom.

"Tiny little thing, isn't she?" Dad said, eyeing the closed door.

"Dad..."

"Which I've always liked too. I admit it. Small women seem sort of helpless."

I had to laugh. "Believe me, Marisol is not helpless."

"Well, you would know."

Oh, for God's sake. "Listen, it's not what you think.

We went to a concert together—we're just friends. It got over late, and she missed the last train to Cambridge, so I said she could sleep here."

"Son, it always starts somehow." Could he be more patronizing?

"That's not what I mean." Marisol emerged from the bathroom just then, stuffing her comb into her backpack, ready to roll. "We weren't sleeping together. Marisol is gay. She's a lesbian."

Well, that was worth waiting for. The old guy took a step backward, couldn't quite get a handle on it, couldn't find the words. "Oh, well. I just assumed..."

"You shouldn't assume," I said.

"...when I saw the jeans..." He sputtered to a halt.

Marisol smiled at me, then let it slide over toward Dad. "Nice to meet you, sir." She stuck out her miniature hand.

"Yes. Of course." He shook her hand. "Welcome here any time," he mumbled.

"I'll walk you down," I said, eager to get away from him, and any dumb questions he might be thinking up, like *Why would a pretty girl like that want to be lesbian?* I'd hate to have to hit him.

We were quiet until we got down the steps. Then Marisol said, "Did we really freak him out, or what?"

I shrugged. "He'll rally."

She poked her usual elbow into my ribs, but softly this time. "It's good you told him the truth."

"I cannot tell a lie," I lied.

"Gio, I've been thinking. Maybe what I'll do this morn-

ing is go to a couple of these secondhand clothing stores I know of. Sometimes you can get clothes that are very funky, but still dressy, you know? That you wouldn't mind actually wearing."

I wasn't following her at all. What did I care about secondhand clothing stores?

"I mean, you know, something I could actually wear to a...prom."

I almost didn't believe I'd heard her right. "You mean it? You'll go with me?" Don't grab her, don't scare her off, I lectured myself.

"Well, you went to Ani with me without knowing what you were in for. How bad could one evening in Darlington be?"

I was ecstatic. How *bad*? It was going to be terrific. A night I'd never forget.

"Anyway, I owe you," she said, taking two fingers and running them across my scar trails, erasing her mistake.

Chapter Ten

"Brian!" I yelled after him as he and Emily pranced down the sidewalk to the parking lot. "It's all set. We're going with you." "To the prom?" Emily squealed. "Yes!" She hopped up and down while they waited for me to join them.

"Marisol can go." I have to admit I was kind of enjoying this little fantasy of Marisol-the-girlfriend, even though I knew it would make her furious.

Brian banged me on the back. "Who'd have thought three months ago that we'd be going to the prom, huh?"

"Not me, that's for sure," I said.

"Not me either," Emily said. "I *never* thought I'd get to go."

"So we need to figure out about the limo and all, before they're all booked up," Brian said.

"Limo? We don't need to go that far, do we?" I could just imagine the look of scorn on Marisol's face if she had to climb into one of those big white hearses. "They're so expensive. Can't we just take your car?"

"Oh, please?" Emily begged.

"*My* car? That piece of junk? Come on."

"Well, then, I'll get my mom's car."

"It's a station wagon, for God's sake. You don't drive a station wagon to the prom!"

"The girls can chip in too," Emily said. "Marisol wouldn't mind, would she?"

I was afraid by now Marisol was regretting consenting to this adolescent ritual anyway; I certainly wasn't going to ask her to "chip in" to ride in a limo. She probably thought she was chipping in quite enough just by showing up.

"Can't you touch your old man for some money? He's loaded," Brian pointed out.

"I don't ask him for money. He gives me some once in a while, but I never ask him. Can't be done." Especially after last weekend. He barely spoke to me in the car on the way home. Mad, I guess, that he looked foolish in front of Marisol. Which wasn't *my* fault. I don't think it's a given

that wet jeans in the bathroom means your son has finally rounded the bases.

"Come on, John. Emily really has her heart set on a limo."

And we certainly can't disappoint Emily. "I suppose I could call down to the Harborside and see if Jake has any weddings this weekend. If he'll take me on both days, I can probably make a few hundred bucks."

I'd waited tables for Jake last summer; it was grueling work—rich people make you take everything back twice—but the tips were great. And it would be the perfect excuse to skip going to Dad's this weekend. Marisol was spending Saturday with Birdie anyway.

"That's the spirit," Brian said, clubbing me on the shoulder again. "I'll make the reservations."

Emily couldn't stand still. "I wonder what color dress Marisol will wear."

"Black," I said.

"You mean she bought it already?"

"I mean she never wears anything that's not black."

Emily's face closed in on itself. "*Never?*"

"Nope."

"Well, you're gonna have a hell of a time finding a black corsage!" Brian said, laughing. Emily joined in, but she looked a little worried. You should worry, I thought. Marisol just might straighten out your sausage curls, and, if you're not careful, she'll take a bite out of them, too.

Dear John (Giovanni),

I really liked getting your letter and the copy of your zine, Bananafish. My favorite piece was the dialogue between Boy and Stepfather; it was touching and funny at the same time. Is it based on reality? (Not that I think it has to be, but you said something about your dad leaving, so I figured it might be.)

I'm a big J.D. Salinger fan too. Don't you wish he hadn't stopped publishing books? Just think of all the wonderful characters we'd have to read about after all these years! I imagine him living in a cabin in New Hampshire surrounded by Seymour and Boo Boo and Zooey and all his other characters—maybe that's all the humanity he needs.

Yes, I've seen Escape Velocity, and I really admire Marisol's writing too. I'd like to meet you both sometime. Which is the main reason I'm writing now. Did you know there's a conference of zine writers being held down here on the Cape in Provincetown the weekend of May 23 through 25? Some of the older zine people are putting it together, but I don't know if the word has spread much beyond Cape Cod. I showed your zine to Bill Murdock, who's one of the organizers, and he said to be sure to invite you and Marisol to the conference.

We're staying in Bill's parents' summer resort, the Bluefish Wharf, which won't be open for business until the following weekend, so bring a sleeping bag if you come. (We promised not to use their linens, but we can put the bags down on beds in the cabins, or if it's warm enough, right on the beach.) Bill has invited some people who'll talk about their writing and how they started their zines. But basically it's just a chance to get to meet people whose work you've read. So far, about forty people are planning to attend. Do you think you can come? Bring more copies of Bananafish.

I really enjoyed reading your letter and doubt very much that you're a genetic jerk. I liked your idea of looking for magic words, even when you don't think there are any. You asked me why I don't let things get me down. I think it's because I've always tried to find my own magic words ever since I was young. That's really what writing is, isn't it? Searching for the magic words. So I guess I'd have to say, this is what keeps me going, figuring out what I have to say and putting it down on paper, word by word.

Hope to see you on the 23rd.

Your friend,
Diana Tree

I was psyched when I got the letter from Diana. Even she thought my writing was "touching." If it was a conspiracy, I was beginning to appreciate it.

The conference sounded like it would be great, and if Marisol would go with me, maybe it would blot out the triviality of the prom the week before. Every time I tried to imagine walking into the Yacht Club with the pathetically eager Brian and Emily on one side and Marisol in drag on the other, the absurdity of the situation made me feel queasy. But then I'd remember the feeling of Marisol's fingers tracing across my forehead, and I'd lose track of everything else, including my ability to inhale and exhale like a normal person. It was weird.

Getting the invitation from Diana gave me a good excuse to call Marisol, who I'd been nervous about contacting since we parted at Dad's front door three days ago. It was like I was afraid I'd made the whole thing up and when I called she'd say, "Go to the prom? Are you nuts? You've obviously got me mixed up with somebody who *likes* you, Gio." Something like that.

But when I finally called, it was her mother who answered.

"Oh, hello, Gio! This is Helen. How have you been?"

"Fine, thank you."

"We were so pleased to hear that Marisol will be going to your prom with you. I'm sure it will be lots of fun!" She sounded like she ought to be Emily's mother instead of Marisol's.

"I hope so." If Marisol had told them about it, it meant

she wasn't going to back out on me. I was sure she'd also tried to tell them it wasn't an actual *date*, but it sounded like old Helen might not be so interested in the fine points of the arrangement.

"I'll go find Marisol for you. I know she'll be so happy you called." It made me sad actually, the way Marisol's mother was grabbing onto me like a life raft. Here she was marching in the Gay Pride parade, flying the PFLAG flag, but still hoping to find out there'd been a little mistake about what Marisol meant by "coming out"; she was really supposed to be getting ready for a debutante ball.

"Hi," Marisol said. "I can't talk long. I've got lots of homework." Her voice was so flattened out I hardly recognized it.

"If this is about that prom thing, don't worry, I got a dress." She chuckled a little. "It makes me look like Spider Woman."

"Sounds perfect," I said, imagining filmy webs hanging from her elbows.

"So, anyway, you can work out the rest of the details."

"Okay." No way was I mentioning the limo. "But I actually called about something else that's going on the *next* weekend."

"What? The Junior Class Wienie Roast?"

This conversation was almost as bad as my nightmare version.

"I got a letter from Diana Tree today. You know, she writes that zine *No Regrets*."

"Oh, yeah, she's the one who's always so happy-sappy.

Nature girl. Why's she writing to you?"

"I wrote to her. I like her zine."

"You do? It's so virtuous! She's a granola-head."

"I don't think...well, whatever. Anyway, listen a minute. She says there's a zine conference on Cape Cod the weekend of the twenty-third. In Provincetown. That's not so far," said he who has seldom left the Boston-Darlington Trail in six years of weekly travel, and has no sense of direction. "Maybe we could go. They're all staying at some guy's resort on the beach. Wouldn't that be fun?"

There was no immediate reaction.

"Hello?"

"I heard you. I don't know, Gio. I'm not much of a group person, you know? I mean, zines are great, but that doesn't mean all the people who write them will be so great. What if it's some big love fest? What if we get down there and find out we're stuck with a bunch of dorks or slimeballs or something?"

"Why would they be dorks? Besides, we can just leave if it's not fun."

She sighed too deeply. "Gio, the thing is, we've been having a lot of togetherness lately. Last weekend, and then this prom thing.... You know?"

Of course I knew. It was the reason I was no longer comatose after an entire life of sleepwalking. It seemed that, all of a sudden, Marisol was necessary to my existence, but, of course, I didn't mention that to her. "We'd just ride down together. You wouldn't have to hang around with me if it's that odious."

"That's not the point."

"Just think about it, will you? You don't have to decide this minute."

"Fine. Consider me thinking. I've really got to go now, Gio. My G and T brain needs to launch an attack against physics. You understand."

I was afraid I did.

"I told you earlier in the week Al's mother had invited me to dinner this evening," Mom said. The annoyance in her voice was probably not caused only by my asking what was for supper.

"I forgot. It's okay. I'll get a pizza or something." She followed me into the den, where I flopped on the couch, attempting to render myself invisible by passing for a normal teenage boy.

"Al said his mother wanted to invite you too, but I told him you wouldn't want to come anyway. We should just leave you alone."

"Leave me alone—that's the way to handle it."

"I'm not *handling* you." That much I knew.

She steamed a little bit, then went in search of her car keys. I turned on MTV so I could pretend to be doing something I didn't want interrupted.

"You could ask Brian to come over if you want. He hasn't been here in weeks."

"He's got a girlfriend. I told you."

"So he doesn't have time for his old friends?"

"Mother! We're going to the stupid prom together next weekend. Isn't that enough? Besides, I'm going to bed early. I'm working at the Harborside all weekend so I can afford this momentous rite of passage."

She twirled the keys around her finger. There was something else on her mind. "I can't help but wonder who this Marisol girl *is*. She just appeared out of the woodwork. You say you met her in Boston, but met her how? On the street? You couldn't know very much about her."

Why was I doing this to myself? To Marisol? One minute I couldn't wait to see her in her Spider Woman dress; the next minute I thought I must be the biggest fool on the planet. It was crazy. In all my classes kids were obsessing about the prom; the girls seemed to think they were going on their honeymoons, and the guys had fantasized some kind of Club Med experience. How on earth was Marisol going to fit into this picture, which, obviously, even included scrutiny from my mother?

"She didn't come out of the woodwork, Mom. She's not a cockroach."

Finally she threw her purse over her shoulder and headed for the door. "I can't talk to you anymore. I'm going to Al's. Don't wait up."

Why? I wanted to ask. Are you sleeping over? But I didn't. One facial blow a week is enough for me. She slammed the door and locked it, just in case this was the moment I was planning my escape.

DEAR MOM,

On the advice of my friend Marisol, the woodwork pest, I'm writing you a letter you will never see. When Marisol writes to her mother, she both blames and forgives her, because, even though the woman abandoned her at birth, Marisol is a fair and balanced person.

But I'm not. I've become warped and crooked in these years since you and Dad divorced, and even though I know you'd put most of the blame on Dad, who does indeed deserve his share, it's you who screwed me up on a daily basis for the last six years. If I did let you read this, you'd put it down right about now. You'd say I'm so unfair. What terrible thing did you ever do to me? You barely escaped with your sanity as it was!

But the problem isn't what you Did do, it's what you Didn't. At first, when Dad left, I was scared, but at least I still had you—(I thought)—you hadn't run away from me. It didn't take long to realize how wrong I was. You were gone too. Sealed up inside yourself where I couldn't get in, never mind that we still lived in the same house.

I'm going to DARE to SAY it NOW—so BRACE yourself—the thing WE NEVER TALK ABOUT: the FACT that you CAN'T BEAR to touch ME, OR HAVE ME touch you. NOT EVEN AN ACCIDENTAL brushing of the hANds, A bump of shoulders, KNEES UNDER the tAble. CERTAINLY NOT the KIND of touching most children HAVE REGULARLY: A HAND ON A FEVERY FOREHEAD, A GAME of tickling, A goodnight Kiss. FOR YEARS I MADE UP EXCUSES FOR you, AND tRIED to CONVINCE myself you didn't REALLY HATE ME AS MUCH AS you HATED DAD. But the EVIDENCE didn't CONFIRM it.

So I TOOK All the SADNESS of the divORCE, ANd All the love I'd ONCE HAD FOR both of you, AND All the FEAR I HAD of bEING AlONE, AND TURNED it iNto A STONE WALL to hide behind. To pROTECT myself. I'm So pROTECTED NOW, DEAR MOTHER, sometimes I FEEl liKE I'm bARELY Alive.

I AM immuNE to EMOTION. AND I HATE you FOR it.

YOUR loving SON,
John

DEAR DAD,

THE LETTER TO MOM WAS EASIER. BECAUSE EVEN THOUGH I'M MAD AT HER FOR LOTS OF THINGS, I STILL WANT TO TELL HER ABOUT IT. SO I GUESS THAT MEANS I THINK SHE MIGHT STILL BE ABLE TO HEAR WHAT I'M SAYING. I DON'T REALLY THINK YOU'LL BE LISTENING, BUT SINCE THIS IS ONLY AN EXERCISE, (OR MAYBE AN EXORCISM?) I'LL TRY TO FIGURE OUT WHAT IT IS I HAVE TO SAY TO YOU TOO.

EVEN THOUGH I BLAME YOU MORE THAN MOM FOR THE MISERIES OF MY GROWING UP, I DON'T HATE YOU. MAYBE THAT'S BECAUSE HATE IS SUCH A STRONG EMOTION, AND YOU DON'T REALLY CALL UP ANY FEELING IN ME AT ALL. WHO ARE YOU? A GUY WHO LEFT HIS WIFE AND CHILD BECAUSE THEY DIDN'T FIT THE SELFISH LIFESTYLE HE PREFERRED. A GUY WHO EATS DINNER WITH HIS KID EVERY FRIDAY NIGHT, BUT HAS NOTHING TO SAY TO HIM. A GUY WHO DIDN'T REALIZE HIS SON EVEN EXISTED UNTIL THE KID BROUGHT A GIRL HOME AND DRAPED HER JEANS OVER THE SHOWER RAIL.

MAYBE YOU'RE MORE THAN THAT. I KNOW IN YOUR SOPHISTICATED, LITERARY WORLD PEOPLE THINK YOU'RE A BIG DEAL. I THOUGHT SO TOO UNTIL I WAS

TEN YEARS OLD. MAYBE SOMEDAY I'll WRITE A brilliant NOVEL, AND THEN you'll WANT to KNOW who I AM, you'll WANT to tEll EVERYbody, "THAT's my SON!"

And I'll SAy, "I REMEMBER you. You'RE the guy I uSED to AlWAyS SEE At BERtucci's ON FRiday NightS. WHEN I had dinNER thERE by mySElf."

           YouR egotiStically NAMED SON,
           JohN FRANCES GAIARDi JR.

Chapter Eleven

I saw the letter on top of the pile of mail on the kitchen counter when I got back from doing prom errands with Brian, picking up the tuxedos and flowers. But Brian was obviously settling in for a while, scavenging through the fridge for bagels and cream cheese, so I tried to ignore it. Why would Marisol send me a letter? I'd be seeing her in a few hours, wouldn't I?

We hadn't had a decent phone conversation since I'd seen her last, that morning at Dad's. She was always in a hurry and couldn't talk long. Yesterday I'd finally gotten her to stay on the line long enough to give her directions to my house, which she didn't seem all that interested in. She kept saying, "I can find it, I can find it."

Finally, I said, "You *are* coming, aren't you?"

"I *said* I'd come. I don't lie, Gio." She sounded furious.

"Look, if you don't want to come..." I couldn't finish the sentence. What would I do if she didn't come? The humiliation of it, and the money already spent, were nothing compared to the pitiful ache I could feel already, in my throat and in my chest, just imagining I might not be with her after all. But then I shook myself out of it. What was wrong with me? Did I expect something momentous to occur at a high school prom? If Marisol backed out, I'd live.

"Let's not discuss this anymore, okay?" she said, a little more calmly. "I'll be there at six o'clock. I'll pick you up, and we'll meet your friends at what's-her-name's house."

"Emily," I said. "You won't like her."

"Can't wait. Gotta run." And that was that.

I realized Brian had been yakking away while he toasted bagels and polished off Mom's tomato juice. He seemed to be praising himself for his taste in corsages.

"Her dress is white, so any color would have been okay, I guess, but the pink roses are really classy, don't you think? I've never seen roses that tiny before, have you? I never even realized roses *came* in so many colors. Did you like the pink the best? I could have gone with the yellow ones, but..." I couldn't listen to it.

"Your corsage is nice too. Kind of dark. I mean a purple orchid on a black dress, but if you think she'll like it."

I didn't really think she'd like anything. She didn't want to come; what difference would a purple orchid make?

Brian was so excited, I was almost jealous of him. He was crazy about that goofy little freshman, and she liked him too. Who'd have guessed *that* could happen? I let him

blab on for about an hour, interjecting just enough verbiage that he believed we were having a conversation. Finally I convinced him to leave so we'd both have time to disinfect every pore of our nervous male bodies before the curtain went up on tonight's show.

At the door he reminded me: "The limo comes at six thirty, but get there before that because Emily's mom wants to take pictures of us."

"Don't worry." I knew I ought to tell him that Marisol wasn't really my girlfriend. Wasn't interested in me that way at all. Was, in fact, gay. I didn't expect her to hide it from anybody, and yet, I didn't feel like announcing it either. It would just come out naturally. That way it wouldn't be a big thing. Nobody would care.

I closed the door on Brian, walked slowly to the kitchen like there was thin ice under my feet, and sliced open the letter from Marisol, my hands actually shaking. It's *mail*, I told myself. What are you afraid of? There was only one sheet of paper inside with a poem on it. A Post-it note in the middle of the page said, "Not for the zine. You'll see what I mean."

I didn't read it right away; I had to calm down first. I was a frigging mess just imagining getting through this whole prom event. In fact, my nerves had been shot ever since I wrote those letters to my parents. Marisol hadn't mentioned that side effect. It was like my skin had all of a sudden been turned nerve-side-out. The letters were hidden under a pile of socks and boxers in a drawer, but I'd have to move them somewhere else or give up changing my under-

wear. Every time I opened that drawer a cold wind shook me like some kind of supernatural force.

The poem was printed out on plain white paper, not decorated like a zine poem might be. No stickers or draw-ings or pictures—nothing playful about this commu-nication. I could tell, by the title and by the timing, this was a poem for me. The last thing in the world I wanted to do was read it.

```
You're Not Listening

I am invisible if I don't
tell you. You'll write my
lines however it suits you.
I haven't lied, but you're not
listening.

I needed your
affection. I didn't think
it would affect me. You
are asking me to change
without a word.

We have in common trusting
no one. I rely on you
to want the wrong things.
You long for the pain
I can give you.
```

Won't be long before I leave
you now we've solved
the initial mystery.
Couldn't we just be
patron saints?

I am invisible if I don't
tell you. You'll write my
lines however it suits you.
I haven't lied; it's time you
started listening.

Marisol pulled up right at six, parked her mother's Nissan
at the curb, and got out. I'd been ready for forty-five minutes, hiding upstairs so I wouldn't have to talk to Mom,
and reapplying deodorant more than once. I'd finally
decided not to mention the poem at all; whatever message I
was supposed to get from it (I'm sick of you?) I could
reflect on later, or she could bring it up herself. I wasn't
going to beg for trouble tonight. Besides, I didn't even feel
like myself in this stupid penguin costume; I felt like I'd put
on some hyperactive guy's personality too. The minute I
saw the car, I headed for the stairs. "Bye, Mom!" I yelled.
"See you in the morning."

"Wait a minute!" She was getting ready to go out to
dinner with Al, just tunneling the final earring through her
lobe. "I want to at least meet this girl."

What could I say? She followed me down the stairs. I

was prepared to open the door to the Spider Woman, or even Morticia Addams, but I was not prepared for the woman who was standing on the doorstep.

"I'm here," Marisol announced without a trace of humor. Except for her voice I might have thought this little apparition was a twin, or merely a hallucination. She was draped in black, or maybe wrapped would be closer to the truth, from the high collar that stopped just under her chin, down both arms to points over her middle finger, around her slim hips and down to her ankles with only a little escape hatch in the back over her heels so she could walk without tripping.

"Wow."

"It's from the Forties, they told me."

"You look like Audrey Hepburn," I said.

She sniffed. "In what? *Breakfast at Wal-Mart*?" She caught sight of Mom hovering in the background. "Hi."

"Hello there. Come in for a minute," Mom said, backing up and making way. She kept pulling on the sides of her hairdo as if she was trying to cover her ears.

"Mom, this is Marisol; Marisol, my mother." I did the intro as fast as possible, figuring to dash out right away, but then I remembered the corsage chilling in the fridge like a head of lettuce. "I'll be right back," I said, abandoning them to each other.

"What an elegant dress," Mom said. "It does look like something Audrey Hepburn would have worn."

"You think so?" Marisol said. "Audrey probably wouldn't have worn these boots with it, though." When I

got back with the orchid, she was sticking her foot backward out of the hem slit to show Mom her old reliable
boots, as scuffed up as ever.

I guess Ms. Van Esterhausen wasn't too sure what to
make of the whole outfit. "Well, you don't really see the
shoes anyway under a long skirt," she said diplomatically.

"Except when I walk," Marisol pointed out.

I struggled to get the corsage out of its box. "Is this
okay? I mean, you don't mind wearing it, do you?" I held up
the orchid.

"Of course she doesn't mind, you silly!" By now Mom
was looking back and forth between the two of us, trying to
figure out what was going on. I guess we didn't seem like
your usual junior class twosome.

"It's nice," Marisol said, forcing a grin to her lips.

"Now, where are you from, Marisol?" The inquisition
had begun.

"Cambridge," she said.

"Puerto Rico," I said, weaving the straight pin around
the flower stem and biting my tongue with the effort.

"He means originally," Marisol explained, flinching as
the pin grazed her skin. The orchid's head flopped to one
side.

"Isn't that interesting?" Mom said. I guess she was too
confused by that answer to ask anything else.

"Shit!" I plunged the pin into my own fat thumb.

"Oh here, let me pin Marisol's corsage on—you go
look in the mirror and get your boutonniere in place," Mom
said. It wasn't until I'd handed her the corsage and dutifully

marched into the bathroom that it hit me; Mom could pin the flower on Marisol, but she couldn't do it for me. I'm not sure how long I stood there staring at myself in the mirror, trying to see if it was visible, the thing that was so repulsive about me my own mother couldn't bear to come in contact with it.

"We'd better go," Marisol called out.

I got the dark red rose pinned on in one try, then walked right past them both toward the front door. "I'm ready."

"It's too bad I don't have any film in the camera to take a picture," Mom said.

"Oh, that would be too much to expect," I said, grabbing Marisol's black elbow and propelling us down the path toward the car. The material was slippery under my hand. Right. Another person I just couldn't grasp.

By the time we crawled into the car, Mom had already closed the front door. No nostalgic waving from the porch for her. She was on to more important things.

Marisol started the car. "What's the matter? You mad your mother didn't take a picture of us?"

I had to laugh. "A picture? She hasn't taken a picture of me since I was a little kid."

"Really?"

"That's nothing." I shook my head. "She hasn't even..." My voice got clotted all of a sudden. I'd never said it out loud, never told anybody, and it seemed like I couldn't. I shook my head again.

"She hasn't even what? What were you going to say?"

I cleared my throat. "Hasn't touched me. Not since I was ten."

"Hasn't touched you? What do you mean? She doesn't hug you?"

"Doesn't let any part of her body come in contact with any part of mine. Like with the boutonniere. She'd never be able to pin it on me. But she could touch you without a problem. She touches her new boyfriend. It's just me. She's crazy."

"That's awful, Gio!" Marisol took her eyes off the road to find mine, but I looked out the window. "I've never heard of anything like that."

"You haven't?"

"Of course not. She's your *mother*!"

"I know. I wrote her a letter."

"You did?"

"Yeah. I won't give it to her though. It's too mean."

"It's good you wrote it, though. It helps, don't you think?"

I shrugged. "I guess. I wrote one to my dad, too. Possibly even meaner."

"Why didn't you tell me this stuff before?"

"I don't think about it that much."

"Well, it certainly explains a lot, doesn't it?"

I snickered. "You mean it explains why I'm so crazy?"

"You're not crazy. Don't let her *make* you crazy! You can't let her!" Marisol demanded. I couldn't promise. I couldn't really talk about it anymore either. Not if I wanted to arrive at this prom in one psychological piece.

We didn't say anything else until we got to Emily's house. I wondered if Marisol was thinking about the poem she'd sent me. Whether it was too mean too. (It was.)

Brian and Emily were already outside the house posing for pictures when we drove up. Brian's mother was there with both of Emily's parents, recording every moment of our glorious departure.

Before we got out of the car, Marisol said, "They do know about me, don't they?"

Here it goes. "I meant to tell them, but—"

"They think I'm your girlfriend?" Her voice rose in surprise.

"You don't have to act like my girlfriend. I don't expect you to."

"I thought the idea of this was to be funny, to sort of goof on the whole thing..."

"I didn't say that." What *was* the idea anyway?

"Well, give me a clue here. Who am I supposed to *be*, anyway?"

"Yourself! Look, I'll tell them right now if you want. 'Marisol is a lesbian. She has no interest in me whatsoever. This whole thing is a farce.' Okay?" I could feel anger heating up my face, but who was I mad at?

"Calm down, for God's sake. You're a mess tonight." We both stared out the window at the yellow ranch house across the street, a kid on a tricycle. Lucky kid: He had years before he'd have to deal with this prom crap. "You don't have to say anything *now*. Let's see how it goes. I won't lie, though—you know that."

Before I could respond, the passenger-side door was ripped open by Mrs. Cookson, Brian's mother.

"Here you are! Come on out! Don't be shy! We want to see you!" She was mercilessly enthusiastic. We had no choice.

No sooner had we closed the car doors than Emily's father turned the camcorder on us. "Hey, you two. Walk over here." The group was assembled in front of a big salmon-colored rhododendron bush. "Smile! Wave!" Mr. Prine directed as he backed across the lawn. I felt ridiculous. Who gets out of a car smiling and waving?

"Hey, John!" Brian yelled, though his eyes were quite busy taking in Marisol.

John. How could I have forgotten about *that* little problem?

While Mrs. Prine arranged us in front of the shrubbery, I introduced everybody. Emily was dressed to look as entirely opposite of Marisol as possible: short, strapless, and all in white except for Brian's pig-pink roses, which were fastened to her wrist like a decorative growth.

"I *love* your dress," Emily said unconvincingly, eyeing the booted hemline. Marisol smiled, but did not return the compliment.

After a beat or two she said, "It takes a good complexion to be able to wear white."

"Thanks!" Emily said, convinced she had the good complexion it took.

"So, here's the mystery woman," Brian said, winking at Marisol. You had to wonder how this could be the same guy

who, a few short months ago, would have swallowed his tongue standing next to somebody who looked like Marisol.

"Gio hasn't told me much about you either."

"Gio?" Brian looked at me quizzically. "You call John Gio?"

She looked at me.

"The thing is, when we met—" I started.

"I call him that—" she interrupted.

"It's kind of a —" I tried again.

"Nickname," Marisol said quietly. And I knew I'd have to pay for the lies sometime, mine and hers, small and white though they were.

"The four of you look over here now," Mrs. Prine ordered. We spent the next ten minutes taking posing directions from both mothers: boys in back, girls in front; everybody in a line; each couple separately; the boys alone; the girls together. (That one was a hoot: tiny Marisol stood on the steps in back of robust Emily like an evil spirit perched on her shoulder or a bad conscience getting ready to whisper.)

I was almost relieved to see the limousine pull up. Emily was ecstatic; the whole family seemed to think this was her wedding. She kissed both of her parents and Mrs. Cookson, too, before ducking into the car. I had a feeling she'd be kissing me, too, before the evening was over if I didn't stay out of her way. The girl was wound up and ready for takeoff.

Marisol had climbed in the car first, always ready to

escape, although in this case I was afraid it might be from the frying pan into the fire.

"Your mother's crying!" Marisol informed Emily. As the limo pulled away we were treated to the sight of Mrs. Prine leaning on Mrs. Cookson's shoulder, dissolved, while Mr. Prine captured it all on tape.

"I know. She always cries at stuff like this."

"Stuff like what?" I asked. "Proms?"

Emily batted at me with her rose-encumbered hand.

"Don't be such a cynic, John," Brian said. "For some of us, tonight's a big deal." He reached for Emily's paw and fondled it in his lap.

"Yeah, John, come on," Marisol said. "You're always such a cynic." I could hardly believe she was willing, at this point, to joke. When she was sure the other two weren't looking, she let her eyeballs roll back in their sockets. Maybe she would forgive me after all.

Chapter
Twelve

Marisol only picked at the dinner, chicken stuffed with something green, and "wild rice," which didn't look any wilder than any other rice I'd ever seen. She refused the ice cream and asked for a second cup of coffee, which she drank with her back toward me, pretending to watch the dance floor.

The Darlington Yacht Club was supposed to have been transformed by the prom committee into *The Love Boat*, of all the asinine ideas. Fortunately their funding was limited, so the decorations consisted mostly of Mylar waves cut out and taped along the walls. Life preservers had been hung every few yards with the markered title "H.M.S. Darlington" curving around the top. Green and blue helium balloons were anchored to the middle of each table by a brick wrapped in blue tissue paper, and crepe paper "bon voyage" streamers hung from the rafters, as though we'd just taken off on our ocean crossing.

There were six people at our table, the four of us and some couple I'd never seen before who must have been such losers they had *no* friends to sit with. Or maybe it was just that they were so tight with each other they never bothered to get to know anybody else. I never imagined sixteen-year-olds could act so married. He opened her napkin for her and reminded her she was allergic to cream. She sampled his salad dressing, then asked the waiter to bring him a clean fork. They were so interested in each other's eating habits, I expected one of them to cut up the other's meat.

But now they were up dancing, and, of course, so were Brian and Emily, though I doubted whether Brian had ever moved to a beat in his life. He and Emily bumped their way through the rock dances, then settled happily into a holding pattern when the band turned slow and sappy. Sitting at the table, not even speaking to my so-called "date," was making me feel like an idiot. Almost everybody was dancing; apparently that's what you *do* at a prom. And we certainly weren't invisible here at our corner table. Marisol had ignited a great deal of interest when we entered the place, and people were still turning around to check on her, as though they expected more of someone wrapped in black than just a stunning entrance.

The thing was, all the other girls were dressed, like Emily, in as little as possible. Most of them looked like they were wearing slips or handkerchiefs. I guess it was supposed to be a sexy look, but on some of them it really didn't work, besides which they looked like clones.

So when Marisol walked in, looking like a tiny Hollywood starlet circa 1942, everybody swiveled to have a look. I didn't mind at all. I felt proud to be with the one person there who had enough individuality to dress in her own style. Of course her proud escort was probably more puzzling to people than her dress; who would have expected Mr. Invisible to walk in with a showstopper?

Not that I was particularly *with* Marisol; she'd hardly directed a word to me since we got here. When she finished cup number two I managed to catch her eye. "You probably don't want to dance, do you?"

"Not really. I'm not much of a dancer."

"Me either, but...look around. There aren't many professionals here."

She shook her head, then turned her powerful gaze on me. "Why did you lie to me about your name?"

I groaned. I'd been waiting for this. "I didn't mean to *lie*. It was the name I used on the zine, and I kind of wanted to *be* that person. I was tired of being plain old John. I didn't think of it as a lie."

"Well, it was," she said.

"I guess. I'm sorry."

"What's wrong with the name John? It was good enough for Berryman?"

"How do you know? Maybe that's why he killed himself."

She didn't smile. "Are you going to call me John now?" I asked.

She made a face. "Can't. I think of you as Gio."

"Good."

She picked up her cup again and then remembered it was empty and clunked it back on the saucer. She was having a great time.

Suddenly she turned on me. "What did you say to your mother? In the letter. What did you say to her that was mean?" Well, that was a leap off *The Love Boat*.

"Come on, Marisol, I don't feel like talking about that now."

"Well, we better talk about something. The only thing we've got together is talking, Gio. You asked the wrong person if you wanted to dance."

She had a point. If this prom wasn't going to ruin our friendship, I'd better try to remember what had made us like each other to begin with. I took a deep breath.

"Well, I guess the worst thing I said was that I hated her. That's how I ended it. It was the last thing I said."

"That's pretty harsh. Did you mean it?"

"Sort of. I don't hate her all the time, just when I think about—"

"The no touching thing?"

"Yeah. You know, what it's done to me and everything. Made me so..." I couldn't say it. I grimaced and clenched my fist in front of my chest.

"Yeah." I knew she knew what I meant. "You put it where she won't find it accidentally?"

"She won't find it. She never goes into my room. It's part of the hands-off policy."

"Would you ever give it to her? I mean, I sometimes

wonder, if I ever did meet my birth mother, would I show her any of the letters. I don't know. Mainly they're for me."

"I probably won't. Although, sometimes I really want her to know how I feel. I want to hurt her back."

Marisol nodded and looked down at her empty cup. "I didn't send you the poem to hurt you, Gio. Just to make sure you know."

The poem. I had almost convinced myself it was just something random she wanted me to read and not a coded message.

"I wasn't really sure what it meant," I said.

"Then you're still not listening," she said, staring straight ahead at a couple of life preservers.

I didn't say anything for a minute or two. The lights were turned even lower than before, which was good. I was glad not to be able to see everybody, or have them see me. Nothing like invisibility.

"I understand some of it," I said quietly. "But why do you say you're leaving me? And what's the 'initial mystery' we've solved?"

She looked down at her lap. "Too hard to talk about it. I'm afraid you'll misunderstand." Her voice had gotten very quiet, as if it were running away from me too.

"I *do* misunderstand. I don't know what's so wrong!" At that moment it seemed as though nobody else was in the room. I just wanted to be with Marisol; I wanted her to want to be with me more than anybody else.

"Gio, my friend," she said, smiling kind of sadly. "You win. Let's dance." She stood up and put out her hand.

At first I felt frustrated that she was willing to dance only because it meant she wouldn't have to talk to me about what was going on between us, but as I stood and followed her onto a corner of the dance floor, that feeling went away. I convinced myself a miracle had occurred: Marisol wanted to be with me the way I was suddenly willing to admit I wanted to be with her.

One of her hands was in mine, and the other reached up to lie peacefully on my shoulder as we began to rock each other slowly back and forth. I forgot immediately that I was at that ridiculous prom. I didn't know *where* I was, just alone with Marisol, her head resting lightly against my chest, her hair tickling my chin, her body moving in sync with mine.

She moved the hand on my shoulder just a little, like a caress. That's what it seemed like. It was so clear; she was touching me instead of saying anything in words. She was *touching* me. Ripples spread out from the spot her hand covered and ran all through my body, electrifying me.

"This is the 'initial mystery,' Gio," she said softly. "Before we couldn't allow anyone in. Now we can."

There were so many wonderful feelings flooding through me, I thought I would burst. This was what people meant! This was what it felt like! I pulled Marisol close to me, put both arms around her, and buried my face in her hair.

I felt her stiffen and pull back, but I held on. "Wait a minute, Gio," she said. "Come on."

I kissed the top of her head and tried to get in a posi-

tion to kiss her face, to work my way down to her lips, but she was pushing me now, shoving me away.

"Gio, for God's sake. That's not what I mean!"

Something was terribly wrong, but I couldn't let her go. I think I knew I'd never hold her again once she got free. She stomped on my foot, her boot heel crushing three or four toes.

"Let me go!" she said, and I had to obey. I suppose there were lots of people watching us by that time, because Marisol was not being quiet.

"This is what I'm talking about! You don't listen to me! We had a nice thing, a good feeling. We broke through something with each other, but you want to make it something it's not!"

"I'm sorry. I thought..."

"You didn't think! You're a *man*!" she screamed, throwing at me the epithet she obviously thought was the worst insult in her vocabulary.

"What's wrong, John?" Brian surfaced and put a hand on my shoulder while Emily lurked behind him.

"I shouldn't be here. That's what's wrong," Marisol said.

"Sure you should..." old Bri began.

"Brian, dear, I am a lesbian. Which your friend *John* knows, but doesn't want to believe."

"That's not fair!" I yelled.

"I'm going now," she said, heading for the exit. "You and your friends can sit here and debate whether or not I'm being fair. I really don't care."

I stood there with Brian, watching Marisol storm out the door.

"She doesn't want to ride back in the limousine?" Emily asked, sounding terribly sad.

That was all it took; I ran out after Marisol. By the time I got to the doorway, she was half a block down the street, her dress hoisted in one hand, boots making good time.

"Marisol, wait a minute!" I yelled.

"Don't follow me!" she hollered back.

"Of course I'm following you," I said as I started running. "You don't even know where you are!"

"I'll figure it out!" She marched on, but slowed a little when I came up beside her. "Well, of course, you can catch me. I'm hobbled by this damn skirt, which I would never have been caught dead in except as a favor to *you*!"

"Look. I don't know what's going on. Could we just talk a minute?"

"*You* don't know what's going on? Where did you get the idea you could suddenly start mauling me?"

Hearing my tender advances referred to as a 'mauling' was more than my ego could bear just then. "What was all that 'initial mystery' shit? What was with your hand moving around on my neck? What am I supposed to think?"

"My *hand* moving...?" Marisol stood there in her majestic dress, little sailboats bobbing in the calm harbor behind her (love boats?), a full moon overhead proclaiming it one of those spring nights people write songs about. Only my girl was livid.

"You think I was leading you on? I've been telling you

since Day One I'm a lesbian. Did you just choose not to believe it?"

"If you didn't want me to think of you as my date, you shouldn't have shown up looking like that!"

That stopped her. "Like what?"

"So...beautiful." I didn't even know I thought that until I said it.

I could tell Marisol wasn't sure how mad a compliment should make her. She stared at my boutonniere for a minute before coming up with a response. "I was supposed to wear overalls and a T-shirt so you wouldn't get confused?"

"I'm just saying, when you're dressed like that it makes it hard to remember you're not available. That's all."

She found where she'd mislaid her anger. "*Available*? And just what did this dress signal to you that I was available *for?*"

"That's not what I meant..."

"Well, obviously it is! I have the crushed ribs to prove it!"

Why was she being so unreasonable? I tell her she's beautiful, and she calls me a pig! All of a sudden I felt my own fuse ignite, burst into flame. I backed up, stuck my finger out at her like (I hate to admit it) a gun, and exploded. "Fuck you, Marisol. Just fuck you!"

For a minute she stood motionless, letting the attack strike her. Then her features tightened into a scowl and she struck back: a stinging slap across my face, and then, before I could move out of the way, another one to keep it company. She backed up.

"I can't believe I ever thought we were friends," she said. "You really fooled me, Gio." I thought there might have been tears in her eyes, but she turned quickly and walked away while I was still testing my jaw for breakage.

I watched her walk away, first thinking: good riddance—who needs this abuse? And then after a minute thinking: She never really understood me anyway. Which rapidly changed to: I never understood her at all. And before long I was watching her small back disappear and thinking: There goes the only person who ever gave a damn about me.

By the time I caught up to her the tears were flowing. Mine anyway. She had more control over hers. (I tried to ignore them. It was so strange; I couldn't remember the last time I cried about anything. Where did the damn things *come* from?)

As soon as Marisol heard me behind her she turned around and started screaming.

"You didn't tell them I was gay! You didn't tell me we were riding in that stupid car! You didn't even tell me your *name*! You swore on J.D. Salinger you'd never lie to me, you shithead, and then you did. All along, you've been lying to me!"

"I'm sorry! I don't mean to lie, especially to you." I tried to take her hand because I felt like I could make her believe me if I could touch her, but she pulled away from me. Another person I couldn't touch anymore.

"First you try to kiss me, then you tell me 'fuck you, Marisol,' which you *know* hurts me..."

"I only said it because you hurt *me*."

"I never lied to you, Gio. If you were hurt it was because you were pretending something that wasn't there."

"Something *was* there! Now *you're* lying. We solved the 'initial mystery'—that's what you said!"

She stopped screaming and slid her fingers up under her bangs like she was massaging her brain. It was a good thing the yelling had stopped because several porch lights had flashed to attention in this affluent neighborhood, and I had the feeling a few index fingers might be warming up to punch 911.

"Yes, okay," she said. "But I meant something else, not...what you think."

"No?"

She took a deep breath and looked me in the eye. "No, not...love. Some kind of deep...connection..." She put her hand over her heart. "Which is confusing. And that's why it has to be over now."

"No! Marisol, I love you!" I said, needing so badly to get the words out into the world, even if nobody wanted to hear them.

"Oh, Jesus," she said, and threw her head back to appeal to the moon for help. "Don't love me, Gio. Don't."

"I can't help it."

She sighed. "Well, now we're really screwed up, aren't we?" She laughed a little bit then, so I did too, though nothing was funny.

She stared out into the harbor for a minute, while I looked helplessly at the back of her head. You could hear a

couple of canine killers scratching and moaning at nearby doors, hoping for a chance to get free and dismember us, but it didn't scare me nearly as much as thinking Marisol would never say she loved me. Finally she grabbed my arm firmly with both her hands, which, for some reason, hurt almost as much as the slaps across the face. "Walk me back to my car," she said. "And let's not say another word tonight."

So I did, and we didn't.

Chapter Thirteen

Brian came by at eight o'clock the next morning. He'd just left Emily at her house, but he was too pumped up to go home and sleep. In a funny way, I was glad to see him. I kind of wanted to talk to somebody about the whole thing, and since Marisol probably wasn't speaking to me anymore, who else was there but Brian?

If I had a normal mother, I might have talked to her last night, since we arrived home about the same time, she from her dinner with Al, me from my aborted prom. Al was just pulling away when we drove up. All I said to Marisol before I got out was, "Can I call you?"

"Let's sleep on it," she said. "I'll call you."

Great. That was the end of that. So I walked in the door, and there was Mom halfway up the stairs already, looking awfully pleased with herself. "Aren't you home early?" she asked me, taking off her shoes on the landing. The question seemed to show a certain lack of interest in the major events of my life.

"No," I said. "The prom's always over at ten thirty."

"Did you have a fight with your girlfriend?" she asked, swinging her shoes from her fingertips like she was eighteen herself. What happened to that person who sat in the dark, uttering monosyllables?

"She's not my girlfriend," I said, passing her on the stairs and heading for the privacy of my own room.

"I didn't really think she was," she said. "Seemed like kind of an oddball with that dress."

"There's nothing odd about her," I said, but I wasn't ready to start fighting again, and Mom obviously didn't care enough about me or Marisol to keep up the conversation.

"Well, get a good night's sleep. You'll feel better in the morning," she chirped as I shut my door on her. What parental concern. That's the kind of all-purpose recommendation you can probably get off a cereal box. "Broken heart? Get a good night's sleep and eat your Wheaties in the morning."

How the hell are you supposed to get any sleep when you've just made a fool of yourself in front of somebody you're crazy about? I lay there wondering about all kinds of stupid things. Whether Marisol had ever seen a guy cry before. What she'd tell her parents when she got home.

(*They'd* be disappointed.) Whether she'd ever wear the Audrey Hepburn dress again. Whether she really hated it that much when I tried to kiss her. How long I could last without a phone call from her before I was totally insane.

It was not a good night. I got up early and had already choked down breakfast by the time Brian appeared at the back door in a badly wrinkled tuxedo. His hair looked like snakes had recently been nesting in it, and there were two hickeys just starting to color up on his neck. His night had obviously been better than mine.

"Man," he said when I opened the door, "what the hell happened with Marisol?"

"I tried to kiss her," I said, coming right to the point.

He leaned back against the refrigerator and stared at me as if he were trying to see inside my head. "How come?" he asked finally. "I mean, she said you knew she was a lesbo, right? Which, by the way, how come you didn't tell me?"

"Lesbian. Not lesbo. I *was* going to tell you. But you're always with Emily now, and—"

"Emily's not prejudiced! You could tell her!"

"Maybe I don't feel like blabbing about my personal life in front of Emily! I hardly know her! Emily is not my best friend!"

Brian pulled off his tie and looked down at it. "Am I your best friend?" he asked tentatively.

I guess I couldn't blame him for not knowing, since I usually act like I'm doing him a big favor hanging out with him. There must be some secret formula for how much to tell people about that kind of stuff. Not too little, but not

too much either. Obviously, it was a secret nobody told me. "Who else would be my best friend?" I said. "You and Marisol. You're my only friends."

He got this loopy grin on his face. "Yeah, you and me have had some good times together, huh?" For a minute I was afraid he was going to give me a hug, but I guess my dour look warned him off.

"So is Marisol real mad at you?" he asked.

"You could say that. I've pretty much destroyed our friendship."

"Just because you tried to kiss her? I mean, it wouldn't kill her, would it? She's not allergic to men, is she?"

I sighed. "It's a long story. You want something to eat?"

He patted his stomach. "I had breakfast at the post prom and then a second one at Emily's. Her mom made waffles and bacon, but they don't drink coffee over there. Could you make coffee?"

I was actually beginning to like the stuff myself. While it dripped through, I filled Brian in on the basics of my story.

"Wow," Brian said. "She wrote a poem just for you? That's so cool."

"Well, it wasn't exactly a love poem. But you're right, she's very cool. I'll tell you, I've never met anybody like her."

"Man, you better watch it. You sound like you're gone on her."

"I am. And the worst part is, I told her."

This last admission rendered him momentarily speechless, but he rallied. "I haven't even told *Emily* that. All these

years, no girl was ever good enough for you, and now the one you finally pick is gay?"

"I know. I'm crazy."

"How could you let yourself do it? If you knew?"

"I didn't *let* myself. It just happened. I can't change the way I feel."

But I *did* feel; that much was undeniable. Even though my stomach was twisted in a pretzel, and I hated myself for acting like such a blubbering fool, there was something else going on too. I also felt awake and alive and, in a funny way, almost lighthearted. It sounds dumb, but I felt like I'd been watching people run past me for years while I was tied up on the sidelines pretending I hated running anyway. And now I was finally untied, free to jump in and join the race whenever I wanted to.

I didn't treat Brian to these metaphorical musings. Instead I let him tell me about his evening, which I knew he was dying to do.

After waltzing themselves into a sweaty frenzy, he and Emily had reached new heights of passion—they'd necked in the back of the limousine for a half hour before going into the postprom breakfast at Dock-of-the-Bay. (Wouldn't it be unbearable to drive limos for proms?) They'd ended up at a table with somebody they knew from *The Sound of Music* who had a flask of vodka he dumped into everybody's orange juice, except Emily didn't have any because she's perfect. Then they'd walked along the beach to watch the sun come up, and ended this flawless evening with waffles and Darjeeling at the Prine homestead. Brian was hope-

lessly happy, which was actually kind of nice to witness.

"Brian. You're here awfully early, aren't you?" The Queen Mother had descended from the throne room.

"I just took Emily home. You know, from the prom." I think he was a little embarrassed at how proud he felt. (The unfortunate zit-blush emerged.)

"Oh, of course. You went last night too. And stayed a little longer than John and his date, I see." She snickered. I held onto my coffee cup with both hands lest it leap out and dump its contents onto her bathrobe.

She turned to me with a smile, though she seemed to be looking inside herself more than at me. "Next time ask a local girl, Johnny. City people think a little too much of themselves, if you know what I mean."

I certainly did, and I wasn't in the mood for it. I know she must be pretty pleased with her interpretation of the events of my life, but she was way off course here. "By 'city people' I suppose you mean Dad, don't you? But I didn't have a date with Dad. That selfish bastard was *your* mistake."

She hesitated just a moment on the way to putting the juice back in the refrigerator, then continued as though I'd said nothing. Brian, however, was spooked. In his family you didn't say nasty things to your parents.

"I better go, John. My mom's probably waiting for me. You know, to hear about the prom and everything." He backed out the door and ran, dragging his tie over the wet grass. I wished I could run home too. But where would that be?

"Have fun with Al last night?" I asked. I knew she

wouldn't speak to me first, after my crack about Dad, so I tried to sound moderately sincere.

"We had a pleasant evening," she said, daintily licking honey off her fingers, not willing to admit to anything as high-spirited as "fun."

"What do you and Al talk about all evening?"

She sighed. "I'm sure it wouldn't interest you."

"No, really. I'd like to know. If he's going to be my stepfather and all..." I stepped a little closer to where she was standing, leaning against the sink, nibbling toast. I wondered if she was even aware of moving an equal distance in the other direction.

"Well, actually, we spent some time last night talking about you, trying to figure out what would make your transition to a new town a little easier."

"What transition?" I shifted position again; so did she.

"When we move to Chesterfield, after the wedding."

"I'm not moving anywhere after any wedding. I told you that."

"John, I'm sorry, but it's time you grew up a little. Other people are involved in this decision, and we *will* be moving." For just a second she let her eyes burn right into mine, then she looked away. "You talk about your father's selfishness, but it seems to me you've inherited more than just his good looks."

That brought me to a dead stop. It seemed like she'd just handed me the last piece to a puzzle I'd been working on for years. She thought I looked like Dad.

"Would you hand me that jar of honey?" I asked,

extending my palm slowly, so as not to startle her. For some reason, I just *had* to do this.

She grabbed the jar by the top so she could place it in my hand and escape unscathed. But I was ready. My large hand, as large as my father's probably, sprang to life and seized the honey and her long fingers all together, one handful, skin to skin.

Poor thing. She was so startled to feel the touch of her own son's flesh, that she sucked in a huge, noisy breath and let go of the honey jar to pull herself away. Of course my interest was not in holding onto something as common as bee pollen; I wanted to know what my mother felt like. As I stood there grasping her taut fingers, they turned cold, and the jar fell at our feet and shattered, a lake of gold spreading out across the clean, white tiles.

It was the panic in her eyes that made me let go after just a few seconds. She jumped back away from me, then pretended it was the mess on the floor she was avoiding.

"Be careful of the glass," she said. "You'd better go out."

"I'll clean it up," I offered.

"No, no," she said. I could see her hands were shaking; she knitted her fingers together for strength. "I'll do it. Go on upstairs."

She was practically begging me to go away. "Fine," I said, leaving the kitchen. "You clean it up. You're the one who couldn't hold on."

* * *

I spent the rest of the morning trying to write. First I pulled up that lame *Memoirs from Hell* article on the computer. Now that life really was hell, it seemed less funny than ever. The only topic I was really interested in thinking about was Marisol, but that was more like not being able to keep your tongue away from the sore tooth the day after a root canal. I thought I'd try writing her a letter, but I was still staring at the sheet of paper half an hour after writing, "Dear Marisol."

I heard the phone ring, but I never answer it, because it's almost never for me. (Before Mom started dating Al, the phone hardly ever rang at all, which was kind of nice.) I heard Mom answer in the downstairs hall, then come upstairs. She knocked on my door and peeked in.

"I think it's *her*. Should I say you aren't here?"

"What? No, of course not."

She shook her head. "You're a glutton for punishment."

"Hang it up downstairs as soon as I pick up!"

I lifted the receiver, waited to hear the other one return to its cradle. "Hang it up, Mom." She did.

"Hello?"

"It's me," the familiar voice said. Adrenaline kicked in immediately; my heart started racing.

"Hey, it's you," I said, struggling not to sound thrilled.

But she was all business. "Listen, Gio. I think we should go to that conference next weekend. We can take the bus down to the Cape Friday afternoon."

"That's great! I mean, you know I want to go." I couldn't believe it. She must not be mad at me after all!

"I know." She didn't sound particularly excited about the trip.

"How come you changed your mind?"

She sighed. "I was talking to Birdie this morning."

Terrific. Now Arnold Schwarzenegger knew about my humiliation. "You told him about last night?"

"I had to talk to somebody, Gio. Who else do I have? Anyway, I mentioned that you wanted us to go to the zine conference, and Birdie said Provincetown is very gay. Lots of gays and lesbians live there or go there for vacations. It sounds really cool."

"So that's why you want to go?"

"Birdie said I need to meet more people like me. I think he's right."

"Birdie said. The word has been handed down from the Bird. So now you think homosexuals are the only people you can have things in common with?"

"It's not just that. Gio, you don't think of me as gay. Which is nice in a way. I mean, you didn't like me *because* I was gay, but it wasn't a negative thing either. It didn't define who I was with you, which I liked. But now I see that was a mistake."

"It wasn't! Marisol! Can't we just forget about last night? I'll never do anything like that again!"

"Gio, come on. How can things be the same again? We can't go backward. It *happened*. Anyway, I think if we go to Provincetown, you'll be able to see who I am in a different way. It'll be good for both of us. You'll meet people too, like that Diana Tree."

"I don't give a damn about Diana Tree! I don't want to meet anybody else!"

"Gio, listen to yourself. What happened to that guy who wasn't even sure if he was gay or straight? Who didn't care? Who didn't like *anybody*?"

I lay back on my bed, exhausted by the whole conversation. "I don't know. I guess he likes somebody now."

"Well, he likes the *wrong* person. Look, Gio, either we go to the conference together, or we don't see each other at all. That's the choice."

Neither of us said anything for quite a while. I thought about just hanging up on her but couldn't make myself do it.

"That's not really a choice then, is it?" I said finally.

"Meet me at South Station Friday afternoon. The bus leaves at four thirty."

"Is Birdie coming?" I had to ask.

"No, he hates zines. Just you and me. One more time."

Chapter Fourteen

I was sure I was going to miss the bus. I'd told Mom the night before I was taking the commuter train into Boston because Dad had a long meeting and couldn't come out to get me. I'd done that before, so I knew it wouldn't set off any alarm bells. I figured if Brian gave me a ride home from school, I could grab my pack and make it to the three o'clock train before Mom even got home from work.

I could have told her about the conference. She probably would have let me go (though she'd have made a big deal about it, calling the bus station, wanting to know when I'd be home, making me promise to stick to some 1950s rules she thought would protect me from life), but leaving without telling her fed into the fantasy I had going that I was running away with Marisol, and might not be back.

I'd told Dad, in the briefest phone conversation on record, that I had to stay in Darlington again this week because Brian's new girlfriend had set me up with a date. The thing Dad found hardest to swallow was that Brian had a girlfriend. Of course, he was ecstatically happy to be off the hook for another weekend, though he made a meager effort not to show it. It was right after this phone call that I addressed the envelope to Marlborough Street and folded my Dear Dad letter into it. I figured he'd get it when he got home from work Friday night, or at least by Saturday, when I'd be long gone.

I probably would never have given Mom her letter if it hadn't been for the honey jar incident. I couldn't get it out of my mind; her straining to get away from me, the look of fear on her face, like I was going to turn around and sting her. I left the letter lying on a pillow in her bedroom and rationalized that, though I was lying to them now to make my getaway, soon enough they'd have to contend with more of my honest emotions than they ever wanted to. I think it was giving out the letters that, more than anything, convinced me I wouldn't be coming back.

I was in the kitchen stuffing an apple into my backpack when Mom came in the back door; I guess I jumped.

"What's the matter?" she said. "Did I scare you?"

"No, you're just home early is all."

"I've got a headache; I didn't stick around today."

If you think you've got a headache *now*, I thought. I had to get out of there before she went up to her room.

"Well, see you later," I said, and headed for the door.

"Wait a minute! You don't have to go already, do you? If your father's in a meeting anyway?"

"I want to get into town. There are some things I want to do...."

She looked at her watch. "You could take the three-thirty train, couldn't you? I thought we'd talk."

Now she wanted to talk! The three-thirty train would barely get me there on time; I'd have to race from the subway to the bus station. But what was my choice?

"Let me just go upstairs and get my slippers," she said.

Out of the question. She'd see the letter the minute she walked into her bedroom. "I'll get them!" I said. "I forgot something upstairs anyway. My...notebook." It never hurt to have an extra notebook.

She was looking at the pack lying on the floor. "It looks like you're taking enough to hike Everest as it is. Don't you have lots of stuff at your dad's already? Why are you taking your sleeping bag? Doesn't he have one?"

Maybe it wasn't so bad those years she was semi-comatose. At least she didn't notice every little thing I did. I was down again with the slippers and notebook in record time.

"I guess he lent his to some friend or something. I like sleeping in a bag; it's easier than making up the bed." Natural born liar strikes again. I promised myself I'd stop just as soon as I cleared things up with Marisol and could start being myself, my *real* self, whoever that might be.

Mom shook her head. "I can just imagine the slovenly bachelor lifestyle you and your father lead together on

weekends." Right. I could just imagine what *she* imagined: The two of us, twin playboys, lounging on sofas with scantily clad young women, champagne corks whizzing around the room.

She put the slippers on and leaned back into the couch. I perched on the arm, ready to leap up and go. "So what did you want to talk to me about?"

"Do you like Al, Johnny? Not as a father, just as a man."

This was what we had to talk about *now*, when there was a bus to catch? I groaned. "I told you, he's all right. I don't know him that well."

"Of course I love Al, but sometimes I get a little... afraid." She drew imaginary circles with her finger on her skirt. "You don't think he'd do what your father did, do you?"

Oh, Jesus. "Mom, how would I know something like that?"

"You know your father. You're a man now. You know how men act."

I was astounded. "Just because I'm a male you expect me to answer for the entire species? Are all women just alike?"

"No, but, men are more...I don't know." She sighed. "The truth is, I find it hard to trust men. Since your father."

No kidding. "Look," I said, "Al seems okay to me, but I can't predict the future. I think you're just going to have to get over this fear thing. It's not exactly fair to Al that he has to take the heat forever because Dad walked out. If you

want to have a decent marriage this time around, I don't think Al's the only one who'll have to work at it."

I can't explain the look on her face. It was like she recognized me for the first time. "You're right, John. You're right. Your father's not part of this relationship. How'd you get so smart when I wasn't looking?"

I felt like saying something mean like, "You haven't been looking for six years, Mom," but she was smiling at me so nicely I didn't do it. All of a sudden I started thinking about her reading the letter, how her face would crumple up. Better not trust me anymore either.

"I've gotta run, Mom. I don't want to miss the three-thirty train too." I grabbed the pack and was out the door before she could get to her feet.

"Have fun, Sweetie. I'll see you Sunday afternoon!" she called after me.

Sweetie? When had she last used a word like that to refer to me? I stopped for just a second while the endearment caught up to me and burned its way into my ears, scalded my brain. Then I started running.

Marisol was standing on the steps of our bus when I came around the corner, her black hair standing out around her head like Liberty's crown.

"Gio! Here! I've got your ticket already!" she yelled to me.

I jumped on, and the driver immediately closed the door behind me and started up the engine. "I wouldn't

have given you another thirty seconds, Buddy," he told me. "I got a schedule to keep, no matter what your girlfriend thinks."

Marisol x-rayed his brain with a glare, then led me back to the seat she'd saved for us. I threw my pack up on the overhead shelf and flopped down.

"How come you're so late? I've been fast-talking that creepy driver for ten minutes."

"My mother wanted to have a chat. And since I didn't want to tell her where I was going, I couldn't say I *had* to leave."

"I didn't tell my parents either. I figure they'll call Birdie as soon as they get worried. He'll tell them I went to a conference, but he doesn't know where it is. That way they won't have coronaries, but they won't find me either."

"Sounds a little bit like a lie."

"Not technically. Birdie doesn't know *exactly* where we are, just the town." I gave her a look. "I know. I feel bad about it, but it had to be done. Escape velocity, you know. They never let me get up any speed."

So Marisol was running away too! Maybe it wasn't a hopeless situation. "Did you think I'd stood you up?" I asked her.

"No. You wouldn't do that to me."

I laughed. "Don't be so sure. As we speak, my mother's worst suspicions are probably being confirmed: like all men, her son cannot be trusted."

"Why?"

"I left her the letter. And I mailed the other one to my

father. So, the cord is cut. I'm free." Just saying it made me
feel like I was floating through space, dizzy from the slow
spin, trying to keep my mind off the ground below.

"You gave them those letters?" Marisol asked. "You
said they were mean."

"They are. Cruel even."

"That doesn't sound like you, Gio. You aren't cruel."

Where did she get off telling me what I was and what I
wasn't? I gave a dark, cruel laugh. "It was *honest*, Marisol. I
told them the truth for the first time. Isn't that what I was
supposed to do?"

"There are different ways to tell the truth, Gio. If you
care about people..."

"I don't care about them. Haven't you been listening
to me?" Man, I felt as crusty as an old barnacle. Who the
hell was she to sit here and lecture me about telling the
truth? A lot of good it had done me to tell her the truth. I
guess all of a sudden I knew for a fact I wasn't running
away with Marisol.

She turned and looked out the window. We were passing the Dorchester Gas Tanks, the dreary outskirts of a big
city, nothing much to pin your hopes on.

"Well, if that's the way you feel," she said finally. "But
nobody's parents do it perfectly. You're mad at everybody
right now—your parents and me, too. But if you run around
trying to hurt everybody back, it just makes things worse."

"Don't worry. I didn't write *you* a letter." I almost
wished I had written her a letter. Why shouldn't I hurt her
back? I was sick of lying in the road letting people drive

trucks over me. I was sore. If she thought she was spending the weekend with a lovesick puppy, she was wrong.

"You can write me a letter if you want...I know how to read between the lines." She smiled her little know-it-all smile, but I turned away and pretended to look out the window across the aisle. I didn't need her laughing at me.

She got a book out of her pack and slumped down to read it, crossing one skinny leg over the other. The bus rocked on, commuters getting off at the stations south of Boston, the sun changing from white to yellow as it descended through horse-tail clouds. By the time we rumbled up and over the Sagamore Bridge across Cape Cod Canal and onto the peninsula itself, Marisol had fallen asleep, her head resting, first lightly, then more heavily, against my shoulder. Though I tried not to admit it to myself, I would have been happy to stay on that bus forever if it meant she'd never move away from me.

Another hour passed. The trees shrank into scrubby pines; roadside motels and shabby clam shacks opened their doors to a few early season tourists. As we reached the Outer Cape, sand dunes rose up on either side of the road, threatening, it seemed, to avalanche over the concrete so one sandy side could meet up again with the other. The road curved once more, and there was a tall tower with a huge blue bay beyond it, into which an orange sun was just dipping. The end of the road: Provincetown.

"We're here," I whispered, hating to do it.

Marisol sat up groggily, embarrassed. "Sorry. You should have woken me. Did I dribble on your shirt?"

"Don't worry about it." I put my crab persona back on.

Marisol asked her pal, the driver, where to find the Bluefish Wharf, and he pointed us down Commercial Street, the main drag, which ran parallel to the bay. It was a very narrow street, busy not only with cars but lots of bicycle and pedestrian traffic too, all vying for the right of way. We passed a woman with feathers in her hair and a large snake around her shoulders, and then a bald guy in a dress. Marisol was so excited, she forgot not to touch me and grabbed my arm. I tried not to know it.

"Look at this place, Gio. Isn't this fabulous?" It *was* kind of fabulous actually: odd and beautiful and wild all at the same time.

We trudged past one brightly painted shop after another: leather, jewelry, secondhand clothes, antiques, hats, T-shirt stores, and art galleries. There were fish restaurants and pizza places, and a number of bars that looked dark and uninhabited. And every now and then, between the buildings you could see a sliver of sandy beach, a fishing boat, an old pier, and always the water, lapping quietly at this little jut of land.

About the time the stores starting to thin out we saw the sign for the Bluefish Wharf. You could tell from a block away that something was going on; there were Christmas lights strung up all over and people were singing along with a guitar. The place itself was pretty funky, lots of little wooden cabins and rooms built one on top of another down the length of an old wharf that stuck out into the

water. Brightly painted buoys and wagon wheels hung off the edge of the deck. At the bottom of some rickety stairs leading down to the beach, the singing group was just breaking up as we arrived.

A tall guy with a scraggly beard saw us and yelled, "Hey, new arrivals! Are you zine people?" He climbed toward us.

I nodded. "I'm Gio...John Galardi, and this is Marisol Guzman. We came down from Boston."

"Right, right. You're the ones Diana invited. I'm Bill Murdock." He stuck out one hand to each of us, so it was more like *holding* hands than shaking them. He was kind of an old hippie type, shaggy-haired, dressed in ratty jeans and an ancient sweatshirt.

"Welcome," he said. "You just missed our campfire sing. We did it early tonight because everybody wanted to go into town and hit the bars. The deal is, find an empty room and throw your stuff in it. There are peanut butter sandwiches and fruit in the office over there. I'm running this thing on a shoestring, so the food is pretty basic."

Somehow campfires, bars, and peanut butter sandwiches didn't seem like they ought to belong to the same weekend experience. We looked around, a little lost. "Let me get Diana; she'll be happy you're here." He went halfway back down the stairs and yelled to a gangly girl with short brown hair who came running over carrying a guitar case.

"These are your two!" Bill Murdock told her, and then said to us, "See you guys later. Gotta find my dancing

shoes." He turned and walked on down the wharf into a room at the end.

Diana sprinted toward us like a big-footed puppy. "Hi! I guess you're John and Marisol. I'm glad you came. I wondered if you would." She smiled first at Marisol, and then, briefly, at me. She seemed nervous, or maybe a little shy.

"Thanks for inviting us," I said.

"This is a great place," Marisol said. "Right on the water."

Diana nodded. "Bill's parents own it, but they don't open for tourists until June, so they're letting us camp out. You wanna find a room?"

We followed her down the creaky deck that passed in front of an odd assortment of doorways of all sizes and colors. Each room had a name plaque tacked over the entrance: Gooseberry, Puddinghead, Pussywillow, Lilliput.

"What do the names mean?" I asked.

"Oh, those are the names of Bill's mother's cats. Past and present. Almost every cabin has a cat name, although she had to throw in a few dogs, down at the far end, when she ran out of cats." Diana knocked on Pussywillow's door and opened it a crack. "Anybody in here?"

"Occupied!" came the shout back.

"Sorry." We moved on down the walkway. "I should have known: Pussywillow is always popular. I don't think anyone is in Pumpkin though." She climbed up a ladder to a second story hut that was perched slightly askew on top another cabin. The view from up there was spectacular: All of Cape Cod Bay sparkled in front of us.

"Yeah, this one's free," she said, ducking her head to enter through the tight doorway. "Do you mind staying in one, or did you want two separate places? It's getting a little crowded already." Her face was devoid of expression; she didn't want us to think it made any difference to her.

I looked at Marisol. There was nothing I wanted more, and probably nothing she wanted less. "I don't care. Stay in one place?" I tried to imitate the careless indifference of Diana Tree, but was not at all sure I succeeded.

"It's fine for now, anyway," Marisol said, dropping her pack and looking around the little yellow room, betraying no emotion. Three little monkeys with their hands over their eyes and ears and mouths.

"So, are you hungry?" Diana asked. She had a way of looking up through her thick fringe of bangs so that she never seemed to be looking directly *at* you. It was a kind of protection, I thought.

"Starving," Marisol admitted. We followed Diana out of Pumpkin and back down to the office, which also housed a small kitchen. She got a loaf of bread out of the refrigerator and a jar of jelly to complement the peanut butter on the counter. "There's not a lot of food here," she said apologetically. "Some people are going into town to eat, although most of them are going to the bars."

"Gay bars?" Marisol asked. She was already spreading a sandwich for herself. I peeled a banana, even though my heart's plummet into my stomach had already filled it up.

"The dance bars are mostly gay, but anybody can go. They're the most fun." I looked closely at Diana. Was she

gay too? How could you tell? There weren't any obvious signs. Maybe that's why some gay people *gave* you signs, like Birdie with his campy chatter, so you didn't make a mistake. Not that knowing had helped me any with Marisol.

"We're not twenty-one," I told her.

"It doesn't matter. Lots of the zine people aren't. As long as you don't try to buy booze, they won't kick you out."

"What are we waiting for?" Marisol said.

"What does this have to do with zines?" I griped. I hadn't come all the way out here to go drinking. Or even dancing. Not that I had come to the tip of this peninsula only to hear the advice of my fellow scribblers either. At this point, I'd have to say my true motivation had something to do with the desperation caused by admitting my future looked as desolate and depressing as my present. Whatever was going to happen out here, I was going to be part of it.

Diana shrugged. "Tonight is just to get to know people. Tomorrow Bill has a program planned. But if you'd rather stay here and read over the zines everybody brought, you can do that." She pointed to stacks of zines on the floor next to a sagging couch. "Or maybe you're tired."

"Oh, no," Marisol said. "Gio's never tired. He wants to go dancing, don't you, Gio? I think we should all go!"

"Okay." Diana looked pleased. "I think most of our group were head for Butterfield's. They have these retro nights when they play oldies and disco songs and stuff. They're great to dance to."

"Let's go!" Marisol couldn't wait to surround herself with other gay people, to show me how gay she could be once she'd ditched me. She wanted me to see her lesbian-ness in action. (Lesbianity?) It was the last thing I wanted to do.

"Lead the way," I said, smiling at Diana.

Chapter Fifteen

I'd never seen any place like Butterfield's. Dark, crowded, and smoky, like you imagine bars will be, but with an enormous dance floor full of all sorts of odd types stomping and grinding to seventies disco music, that dramatic stuff with the beat so heavy it's like a punch in the gut. There were men dancing with men and women dancing with women—that was no shock—but there were also couples that I couldn't have guessed *what* the gender combination was. Half the clientele were pierced, dyed, moussed, muscled, and tattooed. I felt like I had a neon sign flashing over my head: NAÏVE STRAIGHT KID.

Nobody paid any attention to us. Diana located a small table where six or seven zine people were gathered, Bill Murdock among them. There weren't any seats left, but Bill jumped up to make introductions. I was standing next to Marisol, but I think I would have felt the sudden magnification of her force field from across the room. There were four women sitting at the table, three of whom stared intently at Marisol, trying to decide if what they suspected was true. For her part, Marisol locked onto each of them as Bill said their names (Sarah, B.J., June) and she couldn't seem to move past them as the other names were announced.

Due to the tight quarters, Sarah and B.J. were sharing a chair. June moved over and motioned to Marisol to share hers. Marisol sat down carefully, cheek to cheek with June, looking just a little shy. Shy? Who was she kidding? There wasn't a shy bone in that body. Was there?

I tried to hear what June was saying. Apparently she'd read *Escape Velocity* and was snowing Marisol with how great it was. Sarah and B.J. were seconding the motion; it was a big hit with the lesbian contingent. (I believe *I* was the first person to tell her how great her zine was, but who was I anyway? Just some straight, untrustworthy *male*.)

"I wish I'd had such a strong sense of myself when I was in high school," June said. I figured she must be in her early twenties. She rested her arm on the back of the chair they were squeezed into and tipped her head in Marisol's direction.

"I'm almost finished with school. Just a few more

weeks," Marisol assured her. "Then I'm free!" In an unusu-
ally girlish way, she flung one arm out to the side and tossed
her head back. She seemed so young and eager I hardly recognized her.

"Do you want to get something to drink?" Diana asked
me. I'd almost forgotten she was there. "You can get soft
drinks at the bar too."

It was more than I could bear watching Marisol and
June flirting with each other. "Do you want to dance?" I
asked Diana. It wasn't an answer to her question, but she
seemed happy with the suggestion, and we moved out onto
the dance floor. I guess I wanted Marisol to see me with
somebody else, see me having a good time without her.
Except she wasn't paying any attention.

At first I felt self-conscious jerking around to that silly
music, but the beat gets inside you, and pretty soon I just
gave in to it and let go. I wasn't ignoring Diana; I could see
she'd abandoned herself to the music too. Her hair flopped
down into her face, and she mouthed the words to a song
I'd never heard before. We were pretty wild, I thought,
although in that crowd, nobody noticed.

It was almost impossible to be heard over the music,
but between songs I asked her, "Do you come here a lot?"

She shook her head. "Not much. I live in Truro, next
town down, and I don't get the car often. Besides, most of
my friends don't like it here."

"Why not?"

"The gay thing. It makes them uncomfortable."

"You don't mind, though."

She shook her head. "I like people who aren't afraid of themselves."

I would have asked her more, but another song started booming. Finally we took a break and got drinks; it was a little less noisy at the bar, which was behind the biggest speakers. It was then I noticed Marisol dancing with June, not wild like Diana and me, but slowly and sensuously, teasing each other, their eyes locked together. I wanted to look away, but I couldn't.

Diana was taking it all in. "Marisol is gay," she said.

It wasn't really a question, but I nodded.

"I read her zine, so I knew she was, but then the two of you...I thought there was something going on. I wasn't sure."

"We're just friends," I said, turning toward Diana and ripping my eyes away from Marisol's gyrating body.

Diana smiled. "She's pretty."

I chugged the rest of my ginger ale. I was beginning to think this weekend could be hazardous to my health. "You know, I'm kind of tired. I think I'll just go back and crash for the night."

"Mind if I walk with you?" Diana asked. "I'm ready to cash it in too."

"Sure. Just let me tell Marisol I'm going." Okay, I admit it was an excuse to talk to her and to interrupt whatever was going on between her and June.

I wound my way between the dancers and stood next to them, but it took me a minute to get Marisol's full attention. "What?" she finally screamed at me over the sound system.

"I'm going back. With Diana." Wouldn't hurt to let her know I wasn't alone either.

"Okay. See ya." That made a big impression. "Oh, Gio!" she called, and I spun around. "I think I'm going to bunk in with June and Sarah and B.J. They've got a big cabin and there's room."

"More the merrier," June said, grinning this better-to-eat-you-with grin.

"So, if you don't want me to wake you when I come in, you can just move my pack down to...which one are you in?" she asked June.

"Queen Victoria. It's underneath Pumpkin and down one doorway," June explained.

"That way," Marisol began, then leaned in breathtakingly close to me so I could hear without her shouting, "if you get together with Diana, I won't be in your way."

"Diana?" I said, blowing my cover. "I barely know her." I guess she was hoping I'd found somebody, too, so she wouldn't feel so bad about deserting me.

"You could *get* to know her. She seems like she might be your type, Gio," Marisol said, smiling.

"And how would you know that?" I said as sarcastically as possible. I'd had enough of her patronizing crap. Let her sleep wherever she wanted to. I turned around to stomp out, and would probably have forgotten Diana altogether, except she was waiting for me and fell into step as soon as we got outside the door.

"Marisol's sleeping in the lesbian tent," I announced, sounding crabbier than I meant to. "I have to move her stuff down to Queen Victoria."

"I know which one that is. I'll show you."

You could hear the music from Butterfield's for a good block down the street, but gradually it faded out. As we got away from the downtown area, the stillness surrounded us like liquid.

"Wow, it's so quiet here, you can almost *feel* it," I said.

Diana nodded. "It has something to do with begin surrounded by the water, I think. There's no place like this."

"You've lived here all your life?" I asked, remembering the details all of a sudden, how her mother had died when she was young. Ten, I thought I remembered. The same age I was when Dad split.

"We moved here when I was six. My dad's a songwriter, which doesn't bring in a lot of money, but you can live pretty cheaply in Truro. He does gardening for people during the season, then takes off to write songs all winter."

"That sounds like a good life."

"I think so. But my older sister and brother don't. They're more like Mom, I guess. They couldn't wait to grow up and move away."

"Your mother didn't like it here?"

"She made a deal with my dad. She'd live here for five years so he could try out the songwriting thing, but then he'd have to move back to Boston with her and teach music theory again. She was a singer; she missed all the concerts and stuff in the city. But she only lived four out of the five years, and Dad never left."

"So what happens to the songs he writes?"

"Sometimes he sells one. Mostly he plays them on the piano or I learn them on the guitar. He likes that."

We'd reached the Bluefish Wharf by that time and stood looking out over the water for a minute. "I'm lucky we were here," she said. "It would have been much harder to deal with her death someplace where I didn't have quiet and water and dunes to keep me company."

It was nice to just stand there in the dark, looking out over the harbor. By now I was pretty certain Diana wasn't gay. As a matter of fact, I had the feeling she kind of liked me, which was nice, but nothing I felt like doing anything about. If I couldn't have Marisol, I didn't want anybody.

"So where's Queen Victoria's hovel?" I asked at last.

"I'll show you."

I followed Diana down the wharf and, sure enough, Queen Victoria was very near Pumpkin. I got Marisol's pack down and tossed it in the door. "So much for that," I said, whacking my hands together nastily.

"June can seem a little abrasive, but she's really nice," Diana said, reading my mind. "She lived in Provincetown a few years ago, before she moved to New York City. I know her because she worked for my dad one summer, in his gardening business."

New York City? Well, that was good. Marisol wouldn't be able to see her that often once we got home. "She seems okay," I said magnanimously.

"You and Marisol seem very...close," Diana said.

I shrugged. "Sometimes." Diana was looking at me so intently, I had to turn away.

"I was really good friends with a gay guy in my school for a while. It was kind of confusing though. I mean, he was

nicer to me than any straight guy had ever been, so, of course, I really liked him. But he'd tell me all about the guys he liked, and what they said to each other—all the details—and after a while I felt kind of...hurt. I couldn't help it. I guess I wanted him to feel that way about me, even though I knew he wouldn't. Finally we stopped hanging out together."

A parable for our times? "Listen, I'm really bushed. I'll see you tomorrow, okay?"

"Oh, sure." She looked embarrassed, and I felt a little guilty for not responding to her story. But what was I supposed to say? *Oh, me too! Boo hoo!*

"Breakfast is at nine o'clock on the beach as long as the weather holds," she said.

"Great." I started up the stairs for Pumpkin.

"If you need anything, I'm in Bullwinkle," Diana yelled up to me. "The farthest cabin down on the end."

Of course, I wasn't really tired; as a matter of fact I was so agitated, I doubted I'd be able to sleep at all, alone in my pretty yellow cell. I realized I should have gotten a zine or two from the stack in the office, but the energy required to get up off the bed and walk down the wharf again was more than I could muster. Instead I dumped stuff out of my pack until I came up with the old copy of *No Regrets* I'd brought along. Of course, both issues of *Escape Velocity* were in there too, but I wasn't that desperate for reading material. No more Marisol tonight.

I opened Diana's zine to her autobiography. Now that I'd actually met her, I could hear her saying the words, not all in a rush the way I'd first imagined these run-on sen-

tences would sound, but slowly, as though the words were just resting quietly until she let them out. I read the last paragraph over and over. "When you live on Cape Cod like I do, the natural elements become important to you...they help you to forgive people for hurting you...people including yourself can never be as trustworthy as nature because people...don't understand how much they need each other...."

Just a half hour before she'd said to me, "I'm lucky we were here," as though the water itself had healed her after her mother's death. I didn't know if I could really buy it, that nature had so much power, but I thought I might be willing to learn what Diana knew.

I lay quietly then for a long time, listening to the breakers lap at the beach, then turn on themselves and run back out to the sea. I imagined Diana in her cabin at the wharf's end listening to the same mesmerizing sounds. I hoped I could hear what she was hearing.

After a while I got up and wrote a poem.

The sun beating in the windows of Pumpkin woke me early. I'd put the sleeping bag on a bed the night before, not realizing I'd wake up with a view. If I just sat up a little, I could look down the sandy curve of Cape Cod as Provincetown turned into Truro, and Truro into Wellfleet, and on down to the bridge back to the mainland. It made me feel far from home, far from my neurotic mother and my self-centered father, and far from the boredom of Darlington. Not only had I escaped, but I'd escaped to paradise!

Of course, thinking about my parents gave me more than a few uneasy pangs. By now they'd read my letters and were probably busy removing me from wills and changing the locks on their front doors. But there was no looking back now; bridges had gone up in smoke.

I didn't read the poem over; I was afraid daylight might rip to pieces what had seemed complete last night. I'd heard Queen Victoria's handmaidens returning from the bar around midnight, but I concentrated on the rhythmic waves and their laughter barely bruised me.

I slept better than I had all week and was starving after my measly banana dinner of the night before, so I got dressed to go out foraging. As soon as I opened the door I could hear somebody playing a guitar down on the beach and several voices singing an old folk song. It was chillier than I thought it would be; the wind was whipping over the water, so I went back for a sweatshirt.

The singers were on to a Peter, Paul, and Mary song as I went toward the office, searching for grub. Bill Murdock must have gotten up earlier than any of us, because the thirty-two-cup coffeemaker had already finished its job, and he was drawing himself a hot mugful.

"Hello there!" he greeted me. "John, isn't it? Just in time to help me scramble fifty eggs."

"Can I get a cup of that stuff first?"

"Be my guest," he said, handing me a mug from the cupboard above his head. "Couldn't sleep with all that singing going on?"

"They didn't wake me; the sun did."

"Her voice is great, don't you think? She's good on the guitar too."

"Who is it?"

"Diana. You didn't know that was her?"

I shook my head. "I don't really know her. We've just written a few letters back and forth."

"Hey, don't knock letters. Sometimes people say more to each other in letters than they'd ever get around to saying in person."

This, obviously, was not news to me, the preeminent hate-mailer in the greater Boston area. "Diana is a terrific person. If she likes you, you've got a friend for life." Bill poked his finger at my chest, which seemed just slightly threatening.

"She's got a nice voice," I said, which I realized was a pretty lame compliment. Then I started to actually listen to it as it came ringing in the open door. She really *was* good. She has the kind of voice that has something more to it than just hitting the right notes, something that makes you want to hear her sing your favorite song the way *she* would do it.

He handed me a bowl and a fork. "The eggs are in the fridge. Start cracking." From under a counter he extracted a large carton that seemed to be filled with boxes of English muffins. "Donated," he explained. "I've got connections."

"Shouldn't we wait until everybody gets up?" I asked. "If they were out late, they might want to sleep late."

"Are you kidding? Those bedbugs would waste this

whole gorgeous day, if you let them. They'll get up all right, and they'll be happy they did."

That was how Bill was, easygoing, but determined at the same time. He had the whole day arranged for us, and we damn well weren't going to mess up his plans. After he roused the whole place for breakfast (with a personal trumpet volley at every door), he explained how the rest of the day would go: In the morning Dean Gunnison, who was kind of a local zine hero, I guess, would talk about how he got started and why he'd decided to put his zine, *Domestic Circus*, on-line. Then we'd get some exercise—a walk out on the breakwater before lunch—followed by everybody reading excerpts from his or her zine. Then we'd take a rest-and-read break (as Bill called it) and get ready for a cookout on the beach. Finally another campfire, and then we could all do as we pleased for the rest of the evening.

The morning wasn't bad. Gunnison was pretty interesting, although a little smug about his computer savvy. The weather was warm by the time we got to the breakwater, and everybody tied their sweatshirts around their waists to hike out to a little spit of beach on the very tip of the land. (If you think of Cape Cod as an arm with a bent elbow and a cupped hand, we walked from the large knuckle to the tip of the pointer finger across a long rock bridge.)

Marisol walked close to June as they picked their way across the rocks, but if I stayed far enough ahead of them I didn't think too much about it. Besides, she was just trying to make a point, wasn't she? I looked for Diana, but she

was talking to a woman I hadn't met, and I didn't feel like making another new acquaintance at the moment. Lunch was more peanut butter, although a crate of oranges had also appeared to stave off scurvy.

The sun was hot by early afternoon, and most of us changed into summer clothes before reassembling on the beach to read from our zines. I'd been looking forward to this part, getting to hear the work and finding out who these people really were.

Sarah went first with a poem about a car accident she'd been in with her mother years before. It was so good people clapped afterward. I was looking forward to reading her zine during rest-and-read.

June was next. I wasn't impressed, but then, I was having a few problems with June. Hers was a long, silly thing about reading horoscopes. I didn't even *get* it. (Although, I admit, it was hard to hear her around the pounding in my ears.)

Anyway, we went around the group like that, and I really appreciated most of the work. Diana read a couple of very funny poems. Marisol read her "Escape" piece (because June *begged* her to, in front of everybody). I had brought down several pieces to read, things that would be in *Bananafish #2*, but that was just to fool myself, so I wouldn't get nervous. I knew what I intended to read. I also knew there was a good possibility I'd regret it later, but this seemed to be a time in my life when I made reckless choices. When it was my turn, the new poem just happened to be on top of my pile.

I'm Not Lying

I am lying in a clapboard shack
the wind blows through. It has followed me
all the way from Boston to this sheltered
harbor where I am less protected than I've ever
been. Invisible as a fish in the ocean
I've tried to listen, to understand the
mystery of two people who could almost
touch, except they have in common trusting
no one. I'm not lying when I say I tried.

I'm not lying next to you
and I never will. There was a night
we needed more than affection,
though neither would admit it.
To tell the truth it couldn't matter less
who wears the pants or the dress, but only
who becomes visible to whom.
You saw me truly, and I saw all you let me;
I'm not lying now, and I hope I never will.

When I finished reading, almost everybody clapped except, of course, Marisol. She sat cross-legged in the sand, her thin, brown legs tucked together so neatly, and stared, poker-faced, out to sea. June was looking at me, though. June looked like she wanted to grab my neck in her teeth and give me a good shake.

Bill heard the phone before the rest of us; he was up and running for the office immediately. While he was gone, the guy sitting next to me, Michael Something, started asking me about imagery, and complimenting my style. He was a real poetry lover.

"Marisol!" Bill yelled. "It's for you!"

She went running past me, kicking up miniature sand storms behind her bare feet. I started to get up; a call for Marisol seemed like a call for me too. But Michael put a hand on my arm.

"Not you. It's for the skinny girl from the dyke den."

I froze. "What are you talking about?"

"Oh, that's what we were calling the room where the lesbian contingent assembled last night. You probably didn't hear them, but I was right next door. Kept me up half the night."

I hesitated for a minute and then sat down. "Right, the lesbian contingent." It hurt my throat to say it.

Chapter Sixteen

The last readers had finished before I saw Marisol again. She was waiting outside the office, leaning against the wall when I climbed up from the beach.

"Who was it?" I asked as I came toward her. Better to put aside for the moment our poetic differences, I thought, unless she brought them up.

She didn't. "Birdie. I gave him the number here in case of emergency."

"So, what's the emergency?"

"What do you think? My parents are freaking out. Their baby's disappeared."

"Did he tell them you were on the Cape?"

"Yeah. My mother apparently wants to call out the National Guard to search for me." She sighed and banged a bare foot against the building. "By the way, my mother called your mother. She went through my room and found your phone number. I guess she figured we took off together."

It sounds ridiculous, I know, but that made me feel so good; obviously I must be a significant part of Marisol's life if her mother assumed we'd be together. "Oh, well," I said, "my mother would have figured out something was up by tomorrow anyway, when Dad didn't drop me off at the appointed hour. What does she care? She's got the house to herself all weekend."

"Your father knows too. Birdie didn't get the whole story, but I guess our parents have been back and forth on the phone since last night."

"They have? Well, at least they know we haven't been kidnapped or anything. I'm assuming your parents would care." I was not overjoyed to notice June hovering in the background, ready to swoop down and cart Marisol off the second we stopped talking.

"I guess I'll call them in the morning, before I leave," Marisol said. She glanced at June. "If there's time."

I heard her say, "I," not "we," but I refused to give it any significance. "We're leaving in the morning? I thought you said the bus left at three?"

Marisol sneaked another look at June, and I couldn't help turning around too. June was smiling.

"Gio, I'm not going back to Boston with you tomor-row. I'm going to New York City with June and Sarah and B.J."

"What? You can't!" I was as shocked as if she'd announced she was about to elope with Birdie. She was *leaving* me, just like that.

"Of course I can." She turned to June. "You know what? I'll meet you back at the cabin later. I need to talk to Gio alone for a minute."

"Okay," June said, grudgingly. "But don't miss read-and-rest time."

"What is this, Camp Gitchy Goomy?" I yelled at her. "She'll read-and-rest when she feels like reading and rest-ing!" Upset as I was, I was glad to see that June looked pissed off as she walked away. I hated her now for certain.

Marisol touched my arm lightly, and it jerked as though she'd hit me with a stick. "Let's take a little walk." She started down the street, and I followed, of course. What else could I do?

"I don't believe you're running off with her," I said, once we'd gotten half a block down the road. "You hardly know her. What's so great about her, anyway?" I hated the whiny note in my voice, like a little kid arguing not to be left behind with the baby-sitter, on the verge of tears.

"It's not June's fault. I'm not even interested in her."

"Then why are you going to New York? You haven't even graduated from high school yet!"

"I've only got two weeks left. I'm a G and T senior with an acceptance to Stanford. You think they won't let me

graduate? My mother's on the board of my school, for God's sake."

"But why now? I don't get it!"

"Because I have the opportunity now. I like these women, and they invited me to stay with them for a while. Maybe I'll only stay a few weeks. Maybe more. I don't know. I have to do this, Gio. I have to see who I am without my parents hovering over me. Or you."

"Can't you do that at Stanford?" I knew I was begging pathetically, but I couldn't stop myself.

"Gio," she said sadly. Her black nails closed a circle around my wrist like delicate handcuffs. "I'm at escape velocity right now. I have to go."

She actually let me take her hand, and we walked on a little farther in silence, then stopped to look at the bay splash up between two beach houses.

"I liked the poem, Gio."

"You did? You liked it?"

She nodded. "It scared me a little, but that's all right. It was true." She laughed lightly. "How did this happen?"

"What?"

"That you're my best friend?"

Her hand felt like the part of me I was missing. "The problem is," I said, "it's hard for me to be your best friend now that—"

"Stop! Don't say it!" She pulled her hand away from mine and stuck it up in my face as if to block my words.

"Even if it's true?"

She didn't answer me. We stood there, staring at each

other for what seemed like ages, her black eyes piercing me, until finally I looked away.

"Let's go back now," she said, turning. I followed, leaving more and more space between us as we walked. There was no more holding hands.

After grilled hot dogs and veggie-burgers (something for everyone) Diana got her guitar out again, and Bill asked her to do some old Simon and Garfunkel stuff. Most people knew the songs and they sang along, but you could hear Diana's voice over everyone else's, leading the way.

I didn't sing. How could I sing? All I could do was stare across the campfire at Marisol, who was deserting me. She was sitting between the pillars of Sarah and June, and I couldn't help feeling they were guarding her. Keeping away the insensitive beasts: men.

How could this be happening? When I looked back to my life before Marisol, it seemed completely blank. Erased. Whited out. What had I done then? Who had I been? Who could I be now, without her? What would I do? Let Brian and Emily fix me up with freshmen blind dates? No, I'd sit alone in my room, writing drivel that nobody wanted to read. Goopy poems that were too embarrassing to print in a zine. Probably I'd be locked in a room over at Grandma's Haunted House; Al would tell Mom, "It's for his own good we keep it locked," and she'd readily agree. Wouldn't want him walking around *touching* people.

I looked around the circle at everybody clapping hands

and singing. Even though I'd been alone all my life, I'd never really *felt* it like this before. I wished just for once I could be at the center, like Diana, who could touch everyone with her voice and hold them close. At some point it was just too painful to watch all those joyful people, so I lay back in the sand, looking up at the stars, and that was a little better. The stars seemed pretty lonesome too.

After a couple more sing-alongs, Diana said she wanted to do one of her favorite songs, one most people probably wouldn't know. It was by a folk singer named Bob Franke who she'd once seen perform. I'd kind of had it with all these warm group feelings, and was about to head for Pumpkin and put my head under the pillow, but when I sat up, Diana was looking right at me, and I knew she wanted me to stay and listen.

"This song is a little bit sad, but beautiful too," she said. "It's called 'Hard Love.'"

Amazing. I would almost have thought Diana knew what was going on between Marisol and me, knew about my whole life, because the song seemed like it was written just for me. The first verses were about growing up in a home where love was hurtful and difficult, and then it segued into something very much like my current messed-up situation.

> "It was hard love, every step of the way,
> Hard to be so close to you, so hard to turn away,
> And when all the stars and sentimental songs dissolved today,
> There was nothing left to sing about but hard love.

So I loved you for your courage and your gentle
    sense of shame,
And I loved you for your laughter and your language
    and your name,
And I knew it was impossible, but I loved you just the same,
Though the only love I gave to you was hard love."

Diana's voice was beautiful, but I felt like the song was chewing me up. I didn't dare look at Marisol. *Hard to be so close to you, so hard to turn away.* I pulled my knees up and let my head fall down on them so that nobody accidentally looking at my face could see the song had, somehow, been written just for me...*I knew it was impossible, but I loved you just the same.* I was not the only person to ever feel so tortured. Somebody had written this song; it had happened to somebody else. It occurred to me suddenly it had even happened to my mother.

"So I'll tell you that I love you even though I'm far away,
And I'll tell you how you change me as I live from day to day,
How you help me to accept myself and I won't forget to say,
Love is never wasted, even when it's hard love.

Yes it's hard love, but it's love all the same,
Not the stuff of fantasy but more than just a game.
And the only kind of miracle that's worthy of the name,
For the love that heals our lives is mostly hard love."

The love that heals our lives. While everybody was applauding Diana and whooping and yelling for another song, that one line kept circling back through my head. I didn't feel healed—I felt destroyed—and still I knew it was true. I slipped away from the group quietly, without a plan, but as soon as I realized I was headed for the office, I knew what I was going to do.

"Mom? It's me," I said when she answered the phone.

"Johnny! Oh, thank God. Where are you?" She turned away from the phone and announced, "It's him!" Al must have been standing right there.

"I'm on Cape Cod. Didn't Marisol's mother tell you?"

"Yes, but *where* on Cape Cod? What are you doing?"

"We're at a conference, but I can't tell you exactly where, because you'd have to tell her parents. I can't tell you anything about Marisol's plans. It doesn't matter anyway. I'm coming home tomorrow on the bus. I should get to Darlington about seven o'clock in the evening."

I could hear some whispers on her end of the line. "Johnny. John," Mom said. "Al and I have been talking, and we've decided it doesn't make sense to move out of Darlington for your last year of school. Al can make the trips back and forth to help his mother when she needs him. We'll stay in our house until you leave for college. How does that sound? Is that okay?" Her voice was thick and wobbly.

"I know I've made a lot of mistakes, Johnny. We never talked about things, and—"

"Mom," I interrupted. "I don't hate you. That's mostly why I called. I'm sorry about the letter."

She burst into tears. "Oh, sweetheart, *I'm* sorry! I know I haven't been a good mother. I didn't know—I thought you had your father. I didn't know until he told me..."

I really couldn't stand listening to the crying; it was making me feel sick. "You've been okay. It wasn't your fault," I told her. But I don't think she heard me. There was some clunking on the other end of the line, and then Al came on.

"John? It's Al. Your mom's kind of upset right now."

"I know. The letter. I'm sorry," I repeated. I was ready for the guy to lay into me, but he didn't.

"She feels...responsible. But as long as you two are talking now, you can fix it. It'll be all right."

He sounded so reasonable, I didn't know what to say. I thought he'd be mad at me for writing all those awful things to Mom.

"Your friend Brian was here most of the morning. He and his girlfriend were poring over this map of Cape Cod like it was going to tell them where you were. He was ready to organize a search party, get out the bloodhounds. That's a good friend you've got there, John."

"Yeah, I guess so," I said. It was funny to think of the four of them, the two perfect couples, sitting around worrying about me like that...even old Emily. Of course she was probably hoping they could rent a limo to come look for me.

"Maybe you could give Brian a call. Let him know I'm...coming back."

"I certainly will," Al said.

"Thanks." I was trying to remember if I'd ever had a conversation with Al before. Not one where I actually listened to what he was saying. He wasn't a bad guy.

"I should tell you, John, your dad is pretty upset too. Angry, I should say."

The hair on my scalp prickled. "Angry? What's *he* got to be angry about?"

"I shouldn't get into it. It's none of my business. Here, I think your mother can talk again now. So, I'll see you soon. Thanks for calling home, John." He was off before I could respond.

"Johnny? About your father," Mom said, her voice low and scratchy now. "He feels you're not being fair to him and—"

"Fair? He's got a nerve talking about fair!"

"I wish I'd known how you felt," she said, sighing. "None of us have done a very good job of communicating with each other."

"Mom, I'm sorry I sent you the letter, but I'm not sorry I sent one to him. I don't care if I never see him again."

"We'll talk about it when you get home. But, Johnny, it wasn't all his fault. I wasn't the right wife for him. I know that now. Sometimes you just fall in love with the wrong person."

What could I say to that? Hard love hits again.

"I should go," I told her. There was a shadowy figure standing outside the door, and I thought it might be Marisol. "I'll be home tomorrow night. Don't worry."

She started to cry again. "Thank you for calling me,

Sweetheart. Thank you..." I hung up, feeling like I'd just scaled an enormous mountain and was too weak now to go down the other side. The office screen door banged behind me, but when I turned around, it wasn't Marisol.

"Are you all right?" Diana asked.

I wish I could say I was happy to see her, but I wasn't; I was disappointed she wasn't Marisol. "Yeah. I just called my mother. It's a long story."

She smiled. "I know. You told me some of it in your letter."

"Right. Listen, I'm gonna turn in now. I'm kind of beat." She stood quietly as I passed her on the way to the door.

"In your letter you didn't tell me you were in love with Marisol."

I would have laughed if I hadn't felt like throwing up. "You didn't tell me you could read minds either."

"It wasn't that hard."

I nodded. "So you know what a jackass I am."

Diana stomped her foot angrily. "John, weren't you listening to my song? I played it for *you*!"

Oh, man. On the one hand Diana made me feel so good, being there and caring about me, and on the other hand I felt miserable that she wasn't Marisol. "I guess I knew you did," I told her. "It's a great song, and you sang it beautifully. Thanks." I considered the short distance between us, how easy it would be to bend down and kiss her. There was no question that she'd let me. But it was impossible.

She smiled and ducked her head in that shy way she had the night before. "John, when you get home, will you write to me sometimes?"

"Of course I will," I said. "Will you write me back?"

She nodded. "I'm better in letters. I can say what I really mean. You know, the magic words."

I put my hand on her shoulder and gave it a squeeze. She wasn't so bad in person either, but I wasn't ready to say that out loud.

"Good night," I said. "See you tomorrow." Tomorrow was as far ahead as I thought either of us should hope.

Chapter Seventeen

I didn't sleep much. As soon as the first sliver of light edged through the dinky curtains, I was up. I had another eight hours—a whole working day—to spend out here with these people, and I intended to make it a worthwhile day. I'd pick up copies of all the zines in the piles in the office and meet as many of the writers as possible. It would be a day to start over.

But I wasn't fooling myself either. I was up early because I didn't want Marisol to escape without at least saying good-bye. For all I knew, she'd *never* come back to

Boston, or wouldn't tell me when she did. By the time there was a gleam of light skimming across the water, I was bundled up against the chilly morning and walking on the beach. I hoped nobody like Bill or Diana would spy me and come out to keep me company, but no one did. A deserted beach at dawn was the perfect place to nurse my feelings of desolation, to let them trot out a little bit, like a kid plays with the breaking waves, then pull them back inside for another close inspection.

I was just beginning to feel the cold when I heard a door slam up on deck. I walked around to see who it was; sure enough, Sarah and B.J. were carrying their gear out to the street to stow it in an old station wagon. I climbed partway up the stairs and waited. June was the next person out the door, looking half awake and grumpy.

"I don't see why we can't hang around for breakfast," she complained. "I'm hungry."

"I told you, I've got a meeting this afternoon," Sarah said. "We'll stop along the way for coffee."

Just then Marisol emerged from Queen Victoria, pack on her back. She stood on the deck and looked around, like maybe she was searching for somebody. And there I was.

"Could we talk for just a minute?" I asked.

"I don't know." She looked a little discombobulated. "Sarah's in a hurry. Let me ask her." She walked quickly over to the other three, and I watched the discussion. June turned around to give me the hairy eyeball, but Sarah nodded, and Marisol hoisted her pack into the car and ran

back to where I was waiting. Seeing her like that, running toward me, as if she was choosing me, really tore me up. I could have screamed. Why couldn't that be the truth?

"Not too long. They're in a hurry," she said.

"Come down here. I don't feel like having an audience," I told her. She followed me down the steps to the beach.

"I just wanted to say good-bye to you. In case we don't see each other for a while."

"Gio, I'm not vanishing," she said, being careful to look out over the water instead of at me.

"No? It feels like you are."

"Gio..." She sighed in frustration. "You *knew* from the beginning..."

"I know, I know. But this isn't the beginning anymore. I didn't mean for this to happen."

She looked me straight in the eyes, one of those looks that turned me into an invertebrate from the first day I saw her at Tower Records. "Gio, you've meant a lot to me. And I'd like to be able to remember this as a good thing. Just because we can't...," she searched for the words a minute and then gave up. "That doesn't mean it wasn't important."

"Was it important?" I asked, needing to hear her say it again and again.

She laughed a little then, trying to lighten things up. "Of course it was! You know you're the only boyfriend I've ever had!"

But I couldn't laugh. Marisol was the first person,

the *only* person I'd ever been in love with. And she was escaping.

When I didn't laugh with her, she swallowed hard. "Okay. I'm going to tell you something, but you have to promise to *listen*, to understand what I'm saying."

"I promise," I said, ready to agree to just about anything for another glimpse of her unguarded emotions.

She looked down at the sand, her ugly little boot digging itself a hole. "I lied to you too."

"What? When?"

She sighed again, as though the news she was giving me was bad news. "When you asked me to the prom, I pretended to hate the whole idea. But I didn't. I was flattered and even...happy."

"You were?"

She poked her finger at me. "*Not* because I wanted to start dating you—are you listening to me?" She glared at me, and I worked to disguise my sudden glee. "Just because I felt so comfortable with you. I almost never feel very comfortable with anybody. I liked being with you. It made being close to someone feel like it might be...safe."

We were both quiet for a minute, but I had to ask her. "Was that the initial mystery?"

She nodded and kicked a chunk of seaweed back into the water. Then, so low I could barely hear, she said, "I even liked wearing that goddamn dress."

Laughter spurted out of me. "You did?"

She smiled her cockeyed smile. "It's dumb, isn't it? I mean, I could wear a dress any time I wanted to, couldn't I?

There is no *rule* that says a lesbian can't wear a dress once in a while!"

"Why, you little phony," I said as I put my arms around her. She returned my hug immediately, her head pushing into my chest.

"Thanks for telling me I looked beautiful. You're the first person who ever said that. If I don't count my mother."

"Thank *you*," I said. "Thank you for...touching me."

In a moment her embrace relaxed. "I'll miss you."

"I miss you already."

"Me too," she assured me, then pushed away and headed for the stairs. She turned around though, halfway up and gave me one last gift. "Hey, I love you too, Gio," she said. "As much as I can."

Then she disappeared.

I didn't go up to watch them drive off. I didn't want to see Mooney Juney tucking herself snugly into the backseat next to Marisol. I stayed down on the beach, hugging myself against the wind and trembling uncontrollably. I was shaking so much that not only were my teeth rattling, but even my jaws seemed to be knocking together. In a funny way it was wonderful.

The sun was announcing the new day by the time I forced myself to go back to Pumpkin to stand under a hot shower and thaw out.

Before long people will be gathering outside for breakfast. Bill will blow his horn in front of all those feline-labeled doorways, and some people will emerge from their

shacks all pissed off that it's time to get up, and some people will come out all jazzed up and happy to get another
crack at life. Diana probably wakes up singing.

I'm ready, I think, to join them. Very anxious, more
than a little scared, susceptible now to anything that might
happen.

Hard Love

lyrics by
Bob Franke

I remember growing up like it was only yesterday,
Mom and Daddy tried their best to guide me on my way.
But the hard times and the liquor drove the easy love away,
And the only love I knew about was hard love.

It was hard love, every hour of the day,
When Christmas to my birthday was a million years away,
And the fear that came between them drove the tears
    into my play,
There was love in Daddy's house, but it was hard love.

And I recall the gentle courtesy you gave me as I tried
To dissemble in politeness all the love I felt inside.
And for every song of laughter was another song that cried,
This ain't no easy week-end, this is hard love.

It was hard love, every step of the way,
Hard to be so close to you, so hard to turn away,
And when all the stars and sentimental songs dissolved today,
There was nothing left to sing about but hard love.

So I loved you for your courage and your gentle
    sense of shame,
And I loved you for your laughter and your language
    and your name,
And I knew it was impossible, but I loved you just the same,
Though the only love I gave to you was hard love.

It was hard love, it was hard on you I know,
When the only love I gave to you was love I couldn't show.
You forgave the heart that loved you as your lover
     turned to go,
Leaving nothing but the memory of hard love.

So I'm standing in this phone booth with a dollar and a dime,
Wondering what to say to you to ease your troubled mind,
For the Lord's cross might redeem us, but our own just
     wastes our time,
And to tell the two apart is always hard, love.

So I'll tell you that I love you even though I'm far away,
And I'll tell you how you change me as I live from day to day,
How you help me to accept myself and I won't forget to say,
Love is never wasted, even when it's hard love.

Yes it's hard love, but it's love all the same,
Not the stuff of fantasy but more than just a game.
And the only kind of miracle that's worthy of the name,
For the love that heals our lives is mostly hard love.

—*Bob Franke*

© 1982 Telephone Pole Music Co.
Used by permission

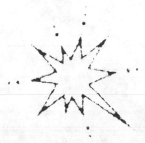